Also by Kirk Scroggs

Tales of a Sixth-Grade Muppet

The *Wiley & Grampa Creatures Features* Series

Tales of a Sixth-Grade Muppet

CLASH OF THE CLASS CLOWNS

Story and Art by KIRK SCROGGS

LITTLE, BROWN AND COMPANY
New York Boston

Little, Brown and Company

Hachette Book Group
237 Park Avenue, New York, NY 10017
Visit our website at www.lb-kids.com

Little, Brown and Company is a division of Hachette Book Group, Inc.
The Little, Brown name and logo are trademarks of Hachette Book Group, Inc.

First Edition: May 2012

ISBN 978-0-316-18314-7

10 9 8 7 6 5 4 3 2 1

RRD-C

Printed in the United States of America

Book design by Maria Mercado

For Kai and Lana

Special thanks to
Steve Deline; Joanna Stamfel-Volpe; Jim Lewis and his band of merry Muppets; Andrea Spooner; Sara Kendall; Diane, Corey, Charlotte, and Candace Scroggs; Harold Aulds; Camilla Dial and Marisa Deline; Mark Mayes; Joe Kocian; Jesse Post and the Disney crew

And a special Sam Eagle, patriotic, twenty-one human cannonball salute to Erin Stein, Maria Mercado, JoAnna Kremer, David Caplan, Jessica Bromberg, Erin McMahon, and the Little, Brown crew. Yaaaaaay!

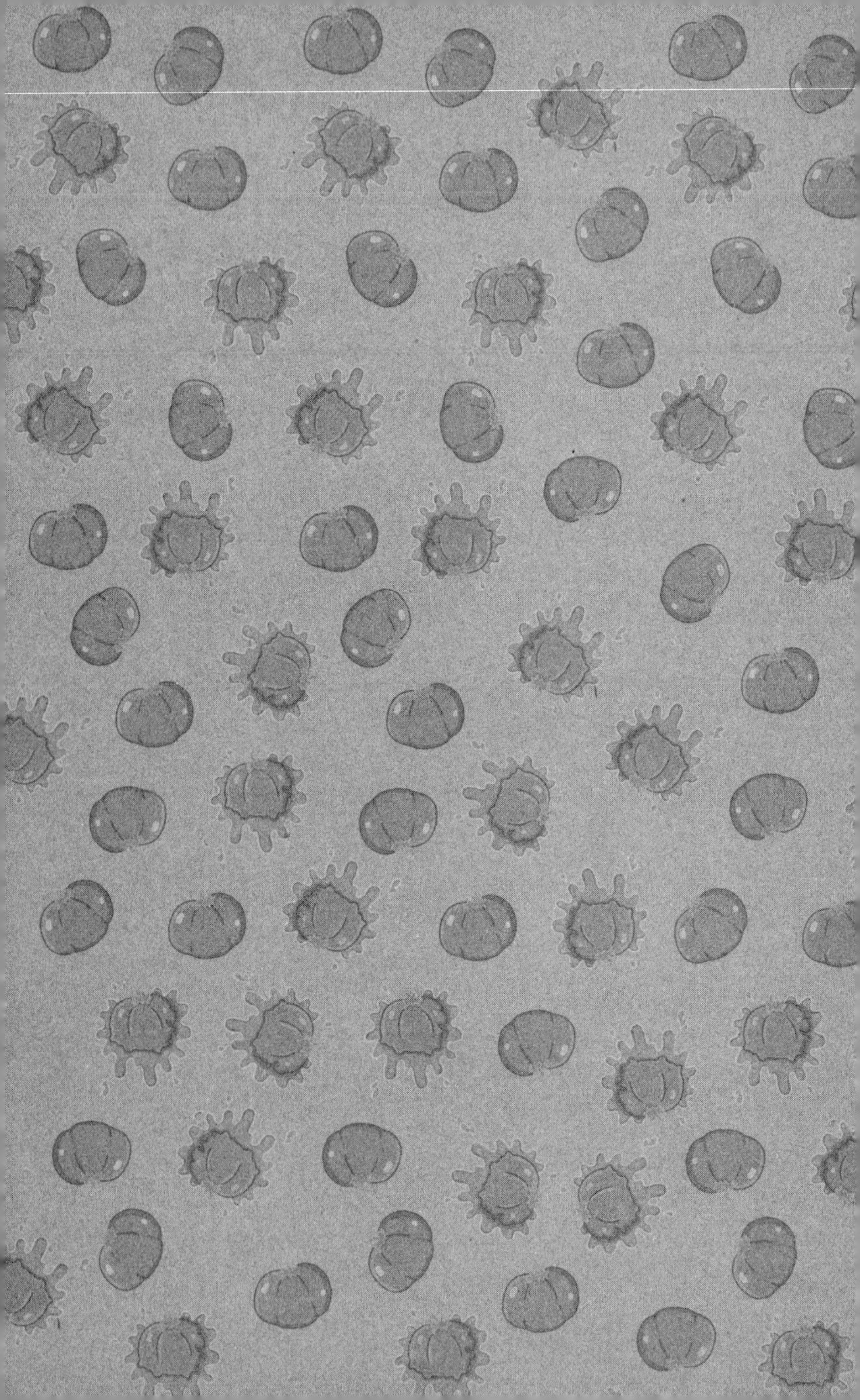

CHAPTER
1
MAINTAINING
FELT
KEEPING YOUR FABRIC SOFT AND VIBRANT!
FELT
Previously on
Tales of a Sixth-Grade
Muppet
by Danvers Blickensderfer
POPULAR STUNTS
ACCORDIAN SHARK RIDING WITH THE
GREAT GONZO
CHEEZY Q's

Previously on Tales of a Sixth-grade Muppet
by Danvers Blickensderfer

Ever since I turned into a Muppet, my life has been pretty hectic. We're talking some major hustle and a whole lot of bustle. Just in case you were too ~~lazy~~ busy to read the first book, here's a rundown of what's happened so far, complete with my own exquisite illustrations:

In the beginning, the Earth was a big blue ball covered with blobby amoebas. Soon the blobs sprouted little hairy legs and crawled out of the slime.... Um, I better just skip ahead or I'm going to run out of room.

Last October 4 I went to bed a normal sixth grader. At 12:22 AM I was jolted awake by a bright green flash, like when you microwave sour green apple Gummi Worms on high heat (don't ask me how I know this). The next morning, I had turned into a Muppet. Even though I had bright orange, fuzzy skin and googly eyes, my family was very supportive.

AAAAHHH!

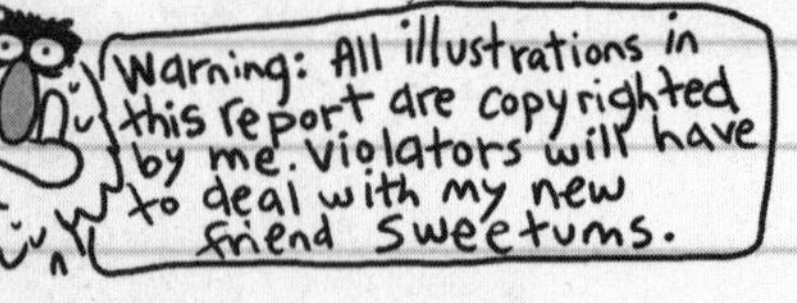

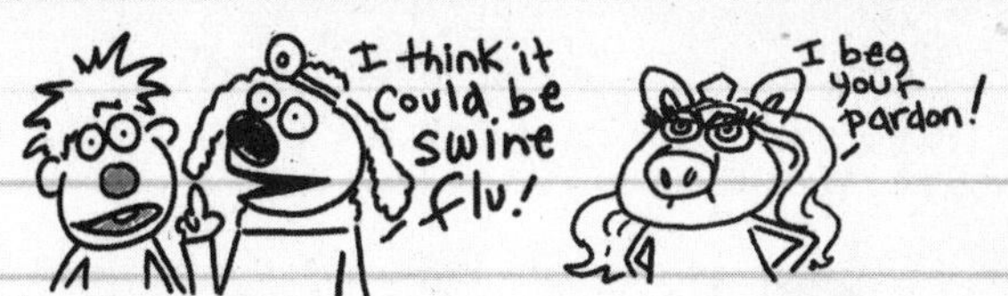

I think it could be swine flu!
I beg your pardon!

DOCTORS were baffled by my ~~predik predicka~~ condition.

But things weren't all bad. I got to meet Kermit the frog and even scored my dream job as the Great Gonzo's personal assistant.

Danvers! fetch me a paramedic!

(In case you haven't heard, he's my all-time hero.) Now I see him every day after school, when I go to my internship at the Muppet theater.

After that, nothing much exciting happened.... Oh! Except that I became lead singer in a Muppet boy band, my evil sister tried to sell my story to the media, I almost lost my best friend, Pasquale, because I was a jerk, and don't forget the big stunt show with exploding melons, saxophone freeze rays, a giant rat, and Dr. Honeydew's fettuccini-powered laser beam (a lot happened—you really should read the book).

leftovers
Zappo!
meep!

So, I'm still a Muppet. Life is good actually. Kids at school are ge
to my new look. My grades are
Everything is peachy kee
been doing some charity
Yesterday, I saved a kit
has never been better
so lucky to have such a loving
Wonderful. Happy happy joy

THIS IS NO WAY TO START OFF A BOOK! WE WANT DANGER AND EXCITEMENT!
YEAH! I'VE READ DICTIONARIES THAT WERE LIVELIER THAN THIS!

Okay, how's this for an opener? It was the biggest night of my life—the fifth annual Kid's Pick Awards at Kermit the Frog's newly remodeled Amphibi-theater. A night of music, megastars, and, most likely, multiple compound fractures. You see, Gonzo and I, along with our super-duper stunt-performing boy band, Mon Swoon, had planned the most dangerous stunt since I made fifty-two jalapeño cheese poppers disappear before getting on the rides at Coaster City.

I peeked out from behind the big red curtain—there was a sea of thousands of people, many of them tween superstars. Little did they know that high above them, perched perilously on a beam and dressed like a giant chicken, was my hero, The Great Gonzo. He was firmly pushing himself back into the world's biggest rubber band, stretching it to the breaking point, ready to snap him directly toward the stage.

COUNTDOWN: THREE MINUTES UNTIL LAUNCH. THE CHICKEN IS COMING HOME TO ROOST.

"All clear on my end," said Rizzo over the radio. He was operating the release lever. One tug and the rubber band would fling Gonzo like a chili burger launched from a slingshot. (Don't ask me how I know this.)

"Affirmative," I answered back through my own walkie-talkie.

I have to admit, I was shaking in my boots. But I wasn't nearly as nervous as Pasquale, my best friend and safety expert. That's him with the protective goggles, rubber gloves, fire extinguisher, 150 SPF sunscreen (custom ordered from Bordeaux, France), first-aid kit, and fire-retardant boots.

"I don't know," Pasquale said, shaking his head. "I've been looking over your diagram for tonight's stunt, and I have to say that—"

"I know, I know...you think it's unsafe," I groaned. Pasquale thinks everything is unsafe, from brushing your teeth to crossing the street to rolling in a barrel full of rusty nails down Highway 620—I mean, sheesh! He's no fun at all sometimes.

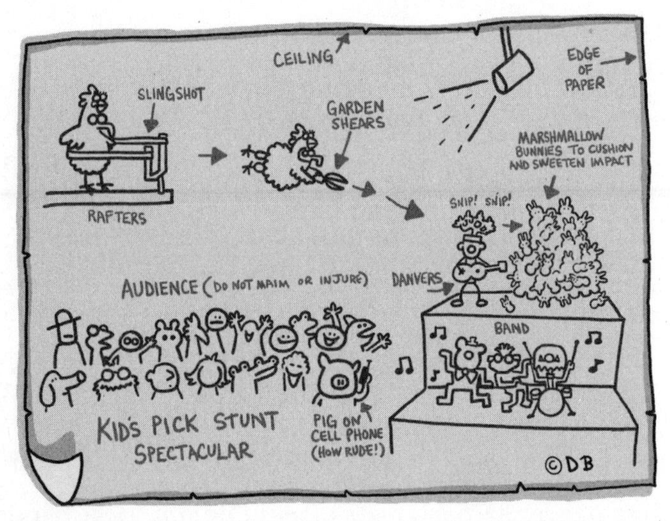

"Pasquale, just relax," I said, patting him on the back. "I'm not the one flying across the auditorium. All I have to do is stand up there, sing my love song, and melt the ladies' hearts."

"While a daredevil dressed as a chicken hurtles

toward your head at two hundred miles per hour with a pair of garden shears!" he added.

"Minor details."

"I agree with Pasquale," said my mom. She and my dad and my evil little sister, Chloe, had been invited to watch from backstage. "Couldn't you just do a nice bowling-pin juggling act, or maybe pull a rabbit out of a hat or something?" she asked hopefully.

"Yeah," echoed my dad. "I hear girls dig it when you pull rabbits out of hats. They think it's really neat-o."

"Rabbits out of hats? Juggling?!" I laughed. "That's child's play. This is a new era of entertainment. People want something fresh, cool, and sophisticated...like giant projectile chickens."

I BEWEEVE IN YOU, BIG BWUDDA. I SAY, BWAKE A LEG!
SAND

"Thanks, sis. I now know that the expression 'break a leg' actually means 'good luck.'"

"If that's what you choose to beweeve, so be it," Chloe said with one of her devilish grins.

Suddenly, Kermit popped his head in and shouted, "Okay, Mon Swoon! You guys are up next. After Pepe introduces you, I'll open the curtains, and you guys hit the stage. Oh, and one more thing—Danvers, Gonzo says that when you see the giant chicken coming at you, duck."

"Got it. Chicken. Duck."

Pasquale handed me my guitar with a worried look on his face. "I hope you updated your medical insurance," he said. "I'm not sure your policy covers garden-shear skewering." I just glared at him until he squinted at me and nodded. "Right, I'm worrying too much. We'll figure it out later...assuming you survive."

"That's more like it." I nodded, clapping him on the shoulder.

"Ladies and gentlemen!" came a voice over the loudspeaker. "Our next presenter has been spotted in swanky clubs and seafood buffets all over the world. He may be a shrimp, but his personality is *muy grande*. Please give a warm welcome to Pepe!"

Pepe ran to the podium, grabbed the mic, and shook his fist in the air, saying, "Okay, I don't know where dat voice came from, but I am Pepe the King Prawn! I am not a shrimp, okay."

OKAY, THANKS FOR WATCHING THE KID'S PICK AWARDS, WHERE WE PICK THE TOPS IN ENTERTAINMENT. PLEASE JOIN US LATER, WHEN WE WILL PICK THE BOTTOMS.

Pepe was having a little trouble with the teleprompter. "Our next act combines tweeny love music with the scary extreme stunts. It's guaranteed to make you queasy, okay. Here is…Mon Swoon, okay!"

I was about to run out onstage with my guitar when Pasquale stopped me, saying, "Don't forget your bonsai hat!" He strapped a big helmet with a bonsai tree growing out the top onto my head.

THE THOUSAND-YEAR-OLD SACRED TRADITION IS THIS YEAR'S HOTTEST ACCESSORY!

CHANGES COLORS WITH THE SEASONS!
JUST ADD WATER AND FERTILIZER!
FROM MUPPET LABS.
THE FOLKS WHO GAVE YOU THE DOUGLAS FIR HAT
WARNING: MAY CAUSE PREMATURE LEAF LOSS IN MEN.

We hit the stage to a thunderous wave of applause as Fozzie Bear and Scooter strutted and did some of their signature dance moves.

I CALL THIS ONE THE *ELECTRIC HIBERNATOR*! WOCKA! WOCKA!

Animal laid down a chill, soothing, groovy drumbeat.

Then I started jammin' on my guitar and singing our latest weather-related hit, "Girl, You Pressure Me So Much, You Broke My Barometer, Yo."

Then, in the middle of the song, I abruptly stopped singing. I turned straight to the audience and announced, "Ladies and swooning teens, I bet you are wondering why I have a tree on my head!"

"We've got something a little more exciting planned for you." I pointed dramatically at Gonzo, perched up in the rafters. "Please direct your attention to the weirdo in the chicken suit above you!"

The crowd gasped as Gonzo continued. "For tonight's stunt, I shall hurl myself toward young Danvers at speeds in excess of good judgment and local traffic laws, while wielding these razor-sharp garden shears, which I will use to perfectly prune the bonsai tree on his head—in accordance with Somoku Kinyo Shu principles, as laid forth in feudal Japan—before landing safely in the mound of marshmallow bunnies behind him!"

"Every show it's the same thing," grumbled Pepe.

HERE GOES NUTHIN!
LAUNC
THE SUPERSIZED SLINGSHOT ROCKETED HIM TOWARD ME AT MACH 1 SPEED.
AAAAAAAAAAAA!
HE ZOOMED OVER THE STUNNED AUDIENCE LIKE A HEAT-SEEKING CHICKEN MISSILE.

I TRIED TO KEEP SINGING, MY SKINNY KNEES KNOCKING.

I felt a disturbance on my head, the kind I imagine you'd feel if you were being dive-bombed by a runaway buzz saw. Then there was a large *crash* behind me, followed by a loud burst of applause. When I turned to look at the mound of marshmallow bunnies, Gonzo was nowhere to be found. In fact, there was a huge hole in the wall in the back of the stage. He had sailed clean through the bricks!

I got on my walkie-talkie, shouting, "Gonzo! Come in, over. Gonzo, are you okay?"

The radio sputtered, then I heard the frazzled voice of the great one: "This is Gonzo, over."

"Where are you?"

"I think I'm in Block City Park. I must have miscalculated the angle of entry. But on the plus side, I managed to trim some hedges and a large poodle on the way over!"

CHAPTER
2

While Mon Swoon exited the stage and Kermit sent out a search party for Gonzo, Miss Piggy was trying to fit into an intricate silver costume for her big musical number, "Seven-Layer Bolero." Her poor assistant, Hockney, was doing his best to help.

"Hmph!" cried Piggy as she finally squeezed into the metallic getup. "There! That was easy-peasy!" She looked like a Spanish conquistador crossed with Cleopatra and a disco ball. Oddly enough, she made it work.

I helped Piggy get her balance. "Cool! What is that outfit made of?"

"I individually hammered more than three hundred pounds of silver serving pieces into battle armor for Miss Piggy," said Hockney.

TALK ABOUT HEAVY METAL!
WATCH IT, BUSTER!

"Ladies and gentlemen," came the announcer's voice again. "You've seen her big blue eyes in your dreams, you've heard her voice in your nightmares...."

"WHAAAAAT!?!" came Miss Piggy's voice from backstage.

The announcer continued: "So now, let's all give it up for Miss Piggy!"

Piggy arrived onstage like a clanking, out-of-control robo-diva. The curtains rose, the spotlight hit her, and she belted out in her angelic singing voice, "Laaaaaaa—"

CRASH!

"Code blue! Actually, code black and blue!" Pasquale yelled, frantically searching for his first-aid kit. "Miss Piggy fell through the floor!"

The crowd went wild.

I ran over and stared into the giant hole that had appeared in the floor. Piggy sat atop a heap of metal and floorboards down below, and she did not look happy.

"Oh, I think I'm going to get a karate chop for this," Hockney said, trembling.

I ran over to Kermit, crying, "What are we going to do? Piggy can't perform like this!"

"Yeah!" shouted Scooter. "And the audience is getting restless!"

"Everything will be okay, okay," added Pepe. "Wait! What am I saying? The show is doomed! We are all doomed! Panic, okay!"

Kermit looked as if he'd been through this kind of thing a million times, which he no doubt had been. But the chaos was definitely getting to him. “Everybody just calm down!” he yelled. “There is no reason to panic! Why is everybody panicking? Stop panicking!”

Did you ever notice that when Kermit gets excited, he’s all mouth and flailing arms?

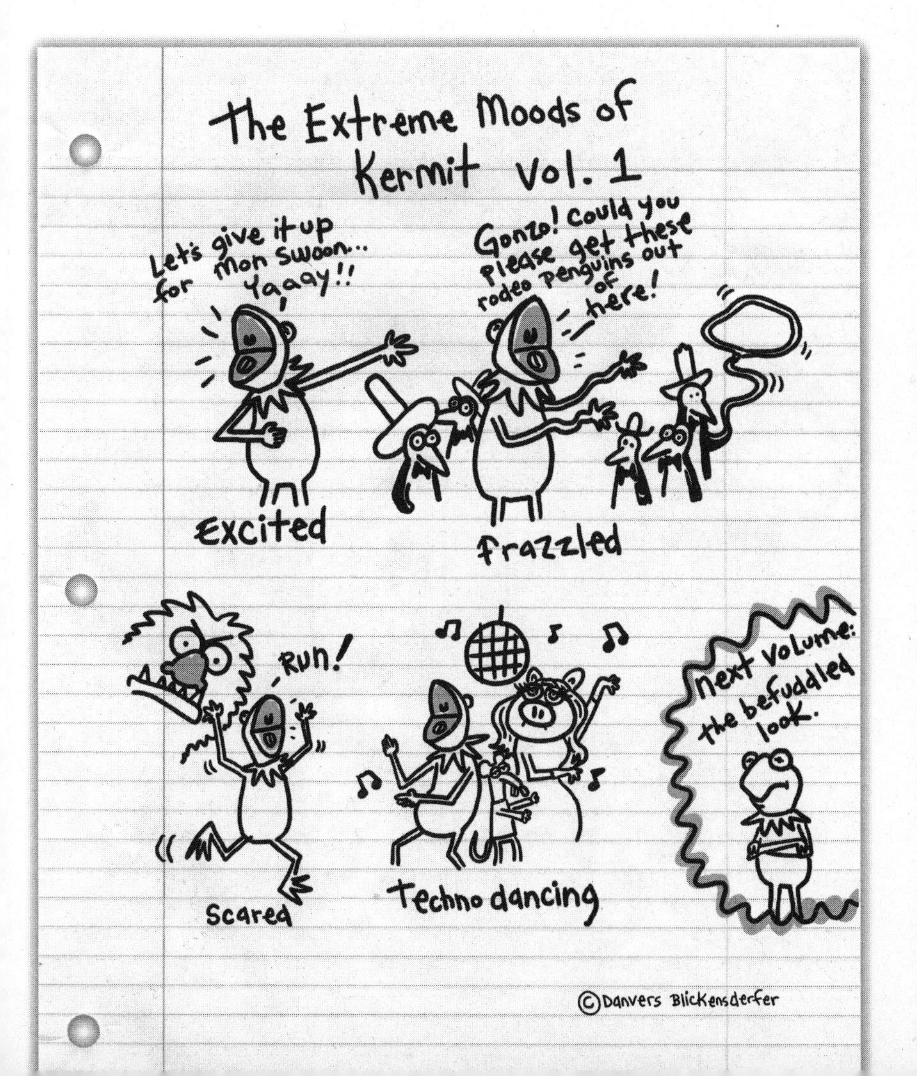

Suddenly, Kermit stopped and said, "Wait! What's that sound? I think I hear singing."

I listened and looked around the room. Yep—I could hear the faint sound of sweet singing, too. That's when I spotted it—my worst nightmare. Chloe was singing "I'm a Little Teapot" for the stage crew in her sickeningly syrupy evil voice. The stagehands clapped for her as she finished with a curtsy.

Kermit ran over to Chloe. I was sure he was going to shoo her out of the way of the crew—this was no place for amateur kid crooners. But before I could see what Kermit was up to, I heard...

"Gaaaangway!" Miss Piggy hollered as she was hoisted out of the hole with pulleys. I had to leap out of the way as she swung out and plopped down on the stage. "Ow! Careful! I'm a delicate flower!"

Rowlf the Dog ran up in his Dr. Bob outfit to render aid.

"Just as I feared," Dr. Bob said, bending Piggy's leg back. "I'm afraid this leg is like a guy that's been hit by a steamroller and gone bankrupt at the same time."

"How's that?" asked Pasquale.

"It's flat broke!"

"Isn't there anything you can do, Doctor?" Piggy asked.

"Well, you're gonna need a soft place to land."

"Why?" asked Piggy.

"'Cause when you get my bill, you're gonna pass out!" Dr. Bob cackled. And then he was gone, which was probably a good thing for his own health.

"Where's my Kermie?" cried Piggy. "Kermie! Kermie! I need you!"

But Kermit was onstage, making an announcement. "Okay, folks. Well, we were gonna do a big musical number for you, but obviously those plans—and that performer—uh...fell through. But we are lucky enough to have a great big bundle of talent and cuteness here to sing you an oldie but a goodie. Ladies and gentlemen, Chloe Blickensderfer! Yaaaaay!"

"Th-this...this has to be some kind of mistake," I sputtered as Chloe bashfully stepped up to her little two-foot-tall mic.

I WOULD WIKE TO DETTICATE THIS SONG TO MY BWUDDA, DANVAS, CUZ I KNOW JUST HOW MUCH THIS WILL WEALLY GET TO HIM.

The audience let out an "Awwwwwwwww..."

"This can't be happening!" I gasped, trembling with horror.

Pasquale reached into his first-aid kit, saying, "I might have a tranquilizer or earplugs in here somewhere."

Piggy took it even harder than I did. Or I should say, the poor paramedic next to her took it harder than I did.

"I've been replaced by a munchkin!" Piggy raged.

"Calm down," said Scooter. "You're in no shape to be exerting yourself."

"No SHAPE?" said Piggy, sporting a look usually seen on angry volcanic tiki gods. "What's wrong with my *shape*?!"

Scooter received the second karate chop of the evening.

Chloe sang the first part of "I'm a Wittle"— I mean, "I'm a *Little* Teapot" a cappella. Then a spotlight lit her up and she growled, "Hit it, boys!"

Suddenly Dr. Teeth and The Electric Mayhem Band burst into a full-on rock-opera version of the classic kiddie ditty as Chloe started high-kicking and belting it out like she was in a Broadway musical.

Chloe finished her big debut with a blast of fireworks, and the crowd gave her a standing ovation.

"Oh, I'm so proud!" Mom said, clapping.

"I feel sick," I moaned.

"Hmph!" Miss Piggy hmphed.

Kermit came back to thank us. "Gee, thanks, Mr. and Mrs. Blickensderfer, for letting us put Chloe's considerable talents to such good use on such short notice!"

Mom and Dad looked a little choked up. I, on the other hand, felt like choking my little sister.

Then Kermit went up to Miss Piggy and said, "And thank you, Piggy. I know it must have been difficult allowing someone so much younger to take your spot...."

"Younger?!" cried Miss Piggy.

Kermit received the third karate chop of the evening.

WHAP!
MAN! THAT PIG SHOULD OPEN UP A MARTIAL-ARTS SCHOOL OR SOMETHING, OKAY.

CHAPTER 3

SPIDER GONZO
Franken-GONZO
GONZO
VIVA! GONZO
GONZO BMX BANDIT!
no Fluffleberries above this line!
LET'S FLUFFLE!
KAI AND LANA IN
TREASURE OF THE GOLDEN RADISHES!

The next morning, I woke up to my blaring siren of an alarm clock and the rustling of my pet rat, Curtis, sipping his usual morning thimble of black coffee and reading the latest issue of *Rat Week*.

My alarm clock read 7:04 as I looked up to see—Aaaaah! Chloe was looming over me with a smile on her face and something behind her back. In case you haven't heard, I have to share bunk beds with my sister, which is only slightly less embarrassing than having your mom walk in on you when you're covered in green Magic Marker and reciting lines out loud from *The Incredible Hulk* (don't ask me how I know this).

"Good morning, big bwudda," Chloe chimed.

"Ugh!" I groaned. "Stop using that cutesy voice! I just had the worst nightmare, and you were in it. I dreamed you sang this horrible song on national TV and became a star."

Chloe grinned like a Tasmanian devil. "Was it a song about teapots?"

"Oh, no," I moaned. "Tell me it really didn't happen!"

"Oh, *contraire*. It happened, all right. Kermit says I might be a huge celebrity someday."

This was not a good way to start off the day. "Get off my ladder," I snapped. "And what's that behind your back?"

Chloe held up her sticky glue bottle and a tube of gold glitter.

"You didn't?" I bolted down the bunk-bed ladder and darted to the bathroom. When I looked in the mirror, I discovered...

"Just because I'm covered in felt doesn't mean I'm your personal craft project!" I bellowed.

"Sorry, big bwudda. When I see felt, I must make it dazzle. I'm a kindergartner. It's what I do."

I had just started to rip off the bits of paper and sequins when a strangely familiar voice blared out,

"No! No! No! No! No! Don't take it off yet! This is good stuff!"

I turned to see Rizzo standing in our tub with a video camera. He even had a film crew with him!

"Rizzo! What are you doing in my bathroom, and who the heck are these guys?" I yelled.

MEET THE CREW OF MY NEW WEALITY SERIES. WIGHT NOW, IT'S CALLED *THE UNTITLED CHLOE PWOJECT*.

"That's right, kid!" said Rizzo. "Your little sis is paying me to document your— I mean, *her* rise to stardom!"

"But she doesn't have any money!"

"We worked that out. Instead of cash, she's given us an all-access pass to your refrigerator!" Rizzo bragged.

I was still doubtful. "But Rizzo, you've never even directed a TV show before."

"That's right," he said. "That's why I brought in the best."

"Don't worry, big bwudda," said Chloe. "He's a pwofessional."

I was fuming at her. "Stop using that voice! You can't just follow me around with a camera crew without my permission! I told you before that I don't want you making money off my story!"

"That's why they're not following you around," Chloe said in her normal voice. "This show's all about me and my rise to the top. It documents the trials and tribulations of being the sister of a brother gone Muppet. It pulls in all the right demographics for a hit show."

"The kid's right," said Rizzo. "Don't worry. We will be invisible. You won't even know we are here."

Suddenly, Mondo spotted Curtis scurrying across the bathroom floor and zapped him with his four-foot tongue!

I snatched Curtis out of Mondo's mouth just in the nick of time.

"How many times have I told you?" snapped Rizzo. "Rats are off-limits!"

"Okay, okay. Sorry," said Mondo. "Make note of dat. Do not a-eat de ratta. He's a-one of de good guys."

CHAPTER 4

MAMMA MIA! DIS A-COFFEE IS DE BEST I EVER HADA!
STILL NO JOBS
JUGO
MICROWAVE

After breakfast, I headed off to school. Pasquale met up with me near the lockers.

"You look irritated—and very sparkly," he said. "Like one of those moody teen vampires."

"It's my sister," I fumed. "Not only did she steal the spotlight last night, but now she's filming a reality show about being the sister of a Muppet. Plus, she thinks she can glue glitter on me anytime she feels like it."

"Just try not to think about her. I doubt anyone was really paying attention to that awards show, anyway."

That's when I was swarmed by a mob of crazed kids.

I SAW YOUR SISTER LAST NIGHT ON TV. WHAT A TALENT!
CAN YOU GET HER AUTOGRAPH FOR ME?
YOU MUST BE SO PROU
WHERE DID THIS CORN DOG COME FROM?

I was almost relieved when the bell rang for the start of history class. At last, I could escape the non-stop chatter about my sis and get lost in one of Mr. Piffle's long, rambling lectures on the Gettybird's Address or Manifold Destiny.

But I wasn't safe even in his class—within two minutes, Button Hauser came up to me with something behind her back.

DANVERS, I MADE THIS PORTRAIT OF YOUR SISTER OUT OF GOLD MACARONI AND DRIED BEANS LAST NIGHT. MAY IT FOREVER REMIND YOU HOW BLESSED YOU ARE TO HAVE SUCH A TALENTED SIBLING.

"Oh, how thoughtful," said Mr. Piffle. "Danvers, what do you say to Button?"

I felt a wave of anger sweep over me, but I kept my cool and accepted the pasta prima donna with the utmost restraint.

ARE YOU ALL OUT OF YOUR GOURDS? MY SISTER IS EVIL! YOU DON'T KNOW HER LIKE I DO! SHE MAKES ATTILA THE HUN LOOK LIKE BAMBI!

WELL, I HOPE YOU'RE HAPPY. YOU'VE UPSET BUTTON AGAIN.

There was an uncomfortable silence in the room.

Then, a snarky voice broke the stillness. "What gives? I thought this was supposed to be history, not drama class."

There were a couple of snickers in the room as I turned to see a kid I'd never seen before sitting in the back of the class. He had curly hair tucked under a funny blue hat, plaid pants, and little round glasses. He even wore a tie with his T-shirt. He also had a big flower pinned to his shirt. Weird.

"Oh, yes," Mr. Piffle said with a cough. "I was just about to introduce our new student. Class, this is Phips Terlington, out of Iowa."

"I'm actually outta ink, too," said Phips. "Anybody got an extra pen I can borrow? Bada boom!"

A couple of kids around him started to giggle.

"Let's all give Phips a warm welcome," added Mr. Piffle.

"Thanks, Mr. Piff*ible*," said Phips.

"It's actually just Piffle."

"Sorry," Phips said, shrugging. "I got a thing for 'ibles' and 'ables' and 'icals'. As in the myst*ical* Muster*able* Piff*ible* and his histor*ical* class*ical*."

I couldn't help but say out loud, "As in these jokes are terr*ible* and intoler*able*."

"I think he's funny," hissed Button. "As in hyster*ical*."

I sat back and watched the rest of class giggle and snicker at Phips's shtick, but I'm telling you, this guy was already working my last nerve.

* * *

After class, I spotted Pasquale in the hall. He was talking with my former mortal enemy, school heart-throb Kip Strummer. (Actually, Kip started out as one of my best friends, and then he became my mortal enemy, and now we're kinda okay again.) Kip was the lead singer of the most popular boy band at Coldrain Middle School, Emo Shun, but they had just released a country album and it wasn't doing so well.

"Hey, Danvers," said Pasquale. "Kip and I were just talking about some new music ideas."

"Hey, Kip." I waved.

"'Sup," said Kip. "I was telling Pasquale that our music hasn't exactly been exploding off the charts in the last few weeks. This country album just ain't flyin', yo."

“Maybe you shouldn’t have let Danny sing lead,” I suggested. Danny Enfant is Emo Shun’s guitarist, and he insists on speaking French even though everyone knows he’s from Bakersfield.

“Dude, you’re probably right,” agreed Kip. “Country just doesn’t sound as authentic when you sing about foie gras and Bastille Day.”

“Well, you’re not the only one struggling in the music industry,” I said. “Mon Swoon has been hurting, too. Don’t get me wrong, Gonzo and I are an endless source of insane stunts, but it’s hard coming up with new weather-related song titles. We’ve been scraping the bottom of the barrel lately.”

Pasquale cleared his throat and said, "I think I may have the solution to both bands' problems."

"We should retire and pour our efforts into growing turnips on sustainable farms?" I said.

"Uh, no...but close." Pasquale shook his head. "I was thinking more along the lines of forming a supergroup. Both bands could record one song together. Mon Swoon meets Emo Shun."

"Hmmm." Kip pondered. "I could dig that."

"Are you crazy?" I blurted. "Pasquale, how quickly you forget! Kip and I have a volatile past, a turbulent relationship, an explosive history!" Literally—during the show we did on Kip's parents' party boat, the *volatile* nitroglycerin I was using for our pyrotechnics show was set off by boat *turbulence*, and a small *explosion* ensued.

"I'm willing to put our differences and near-death experiences aside," said Kip, extending his hand to shake. "Come on, it's only for one song. I've realized that our friendship is as important as ever since your...uh...*incident*."

I gave Kip a dirty look. "'Incident'?"

"You know, your... *transformation.*"

I was steamed. "You mean ever since I turned into a Muppet?"

"Well, uh..."

"Let me tell you something, buster—I don't need your sympathy because I'm a Muppet! Being a Muppet happens to be great!"

YOU CERTAINLY WON'T GET ANY SYMPATHY FROM US!

Kip put his hands up, trying to calm me down. "Look, dude. Don't get bent out of shape."

"*Bent* out of shape?!" I yelled. "Are you, by chance, referring to my bendy, wobbly Muppet arms and legs?"

"Oh, brother," moaned Pasquale.

But I wasn't finished. "Kip, just go back to your sickeningly sappy boy band and let Mon Swoon take care of creating the *real* music! All you care about is your hair and impressing girls, anyway!"

"Now hold on a minute!" snapped Kip. "There's a lot more to me than my super-stylish auburn hair and impressing girls— Hey!" Kip abruptly interrupted himself and looked around the hallway. "Where are the girls? I've been standing out here for ten minutes now, and there's not a lovely lady to be found. Usually they're all over me."

Suddenly, the other two members of Emo Shun, Danny Enfant and Cody Carter, ran up to us.

"Kip!" cried Cody. "You gotta see this new kid! He's surrounded by girls!"

"Ce *bouffon!*" cried Danny. "Ce *comédien!*"

We all scooted down the hall to where a big group of kids was gathered around the new guy, Phips Terlington. Everyone was cracking up and clapping.

Phips was picking a ukulele, blowing a harmonica, and painting a portrait of Ben Franklin with his big toe.

THEY CALL ME VINCENT VAN TOE! GET IT—VAN *TOE*?
TOE PAINT

When Phips saw us walk up, he stopped playing and shouted, "Hey! It's the bedazz*ible* boy Muppet! I got a question for ya, Dampers."

"It's Danvers," I grumbled.

Suddenly, Phips squirted me in the face with the fake flower on his shirt. "Well, you're definitely damper now!"

The kids in the hallway went nuts with laughter.

Then the one-boy boy band turned his sights on Kip. "Hey, you must be Kipple, the lead singer of Emo Shun!" His voice turned deep as he did a dead-on Kip impression: "Uh, like, dude, I dig your tunage. Your music has, like, helped me through many a sleepless night, no joke. I just play those romantic jams of yours and I'm out like a light, yo."

"Uh, thanks, I guess," said Kip, not realizing that everyone in the hall was snickering at him.

"Hey, no problem*able*. I got one last question for you guys," snarked Phips, pulling a tomato out of his locker. "Whaddaya get when you play catch with a ripe tomato?"

"I don't know," said Pasquale.

Phips hurled the tomato and it hit Pasquale in the head, splattering us bystanders with red mush.

"Catch-*up*!" Phips shouted while everyone hooted and howled with glee.

Phips gave me a friendly nudge in the shoulder, then walked away. "You know I'm just kidding. We're cool, right?"

THIS DUDE'S GOTTA GO.
EVEN MOSQUITOES WOULD FIND HIM ANNOYING.
HMMMMPH.

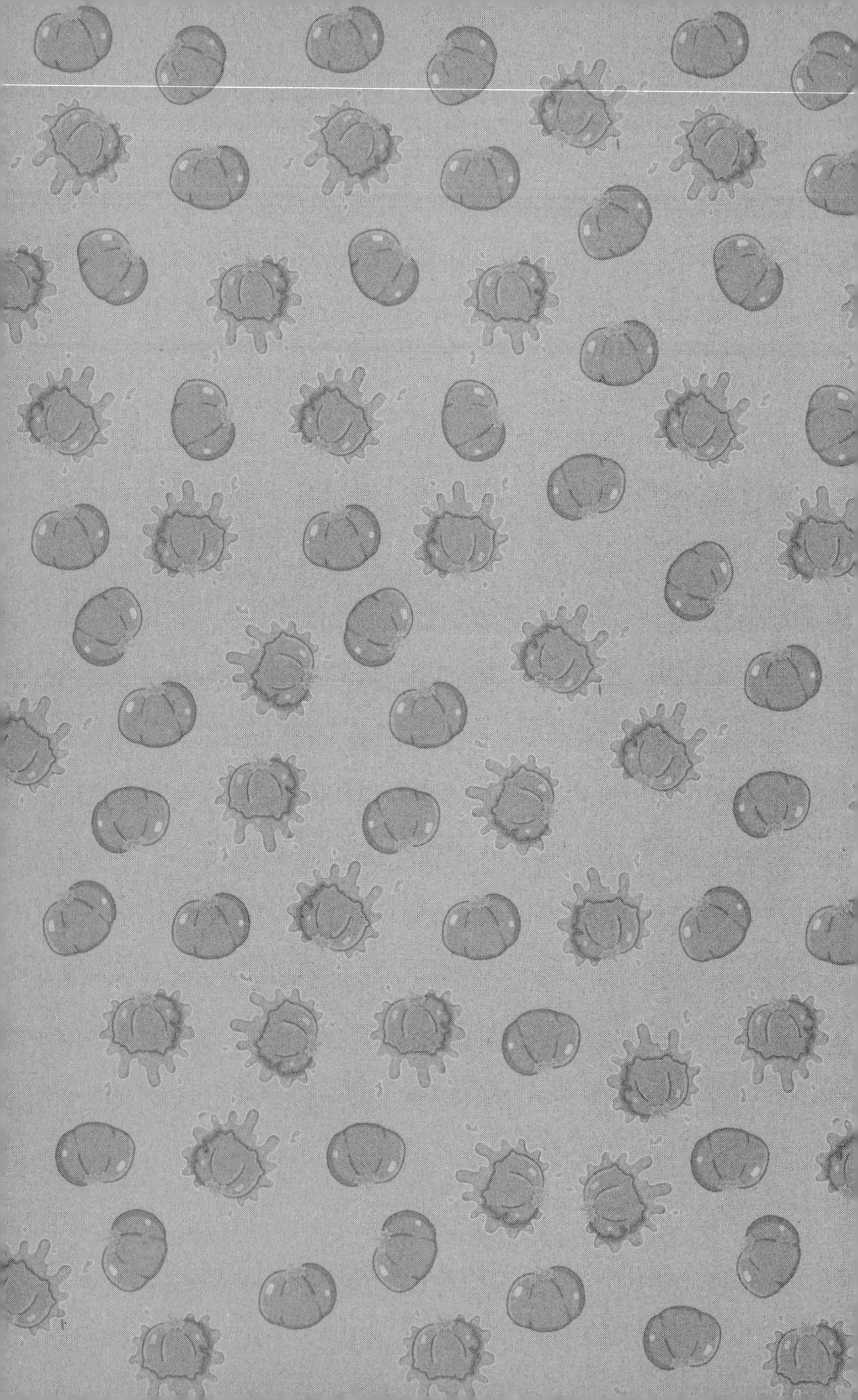

CHAPTER 5

After school, Pasquale and I headed over to our internships at the Muppet Theater. It was my favorite place in the world. A place where I could relax.

Engage in intellectual conversation.

Get some peace and quiet.

And escape all the doom and gloom in the world.

But on this particular day, the theater wasn't all that quiet.

Gonzo and I had come up with a stunt-and-sound spectacular that would make everything else we had done look like a game of ring-around-the-rosy.

This bedbug-yodeling catfish stunt was going to be so dangerous and bold that Pasquale had designed a computer program to determine if it was even possible.

I'VE PLUGGED ALL THE DATA AND STUNT PARAMETERS INTO THE DAREDEVIL X150, AND NOW IT WILL DISPLAY ITS SCIENTIFIC CONCLUSION.

"That's great!" shouted Gonzo. "That means this stunt is guaranteed to be incredible!"

Suddenly, Fozzie, Scooter, and Pepe burst in, all of them playing games on their phones.

"Guys, take a look at this!" shouted Fozzie. "Scooter designed a video game based on our stunt at the Kid's Pick Awards last night!"

"We could make millions off of this, okay," said Pepe, "and maybe even some money, too."

"This is terrrrrrrific!" Gonzo cried.

The game looked awesome. "Wow!" I said. "There's Gonzo in his giant chicken outfit. And there's me, singing an actual Mon Swoon single!"

"Yeah!" said Pepe. "And, unlike real life, you can turn the volume down on the sappy love songs, okay!"

We all gave Pepe a dirty look.

"Oops!" He gulped. "Did I say that out loud?"

"What's the object of the game?" I asked.

"To hurl the daredevil in the chicken suit and pick off as many Mon Swoon band members as possible," said Fozzie. "It's called Angry Chickens."

Pasquale frowned. “I don’t know. Sounds too similar to Perturbed Birds, if you ask me. There might be legal ramifications.”

“And lawsuits, too, okay,” added Pepe.

“Criminy! He’s right,” said Scooter. “We’ll have to change the name. How about Hacked-Off Hens?”

“Or Grumpy Grackles?” I added.

Suddenly, we heard the sound of crashing glass and someone shrieking, “Whaaaaaattt?” from outside Gonzo’s dressing room.

I knew that sound. It was either the sound of a stampede of angry triceratops, or...gulp...Miss Piggy!

OR MAYBE INSTEAD OF THE ANGRY CHICKEN, YOU CAN HURL THE STUDLY BRAVE KING PRAWN INTO THE ARMS OF HIS ADORING LADY FANS, OKAY. WE CAN CALL IT SUPER-SMOOTH KING PRAWN EXPLOSION OF BRAVERY OR SOMETHING LIKE THAT...AND I WOULD GET ALL OF THE PROFITS, OKAY.

CHAPTER

I'M VEWY HONORED TO MEET SUCH A HUUUUGE MOVIE STAR WHO'S BEEN IN THE BUSINESS FOR SOOOOOO LONG.
PIGGY ♥'s KERMIE

When we ran out of the office, we discovered the source of all the commotion: Miss Piggy was throwing a Grade A temper tantrum, rolling around backstage in her wheelchair, ramming walls with her gigantic cast, which was sticking out in front of her like a battering ram.

"*Moi* will not be replaced by some toddler troubadour!" Piggy huffed.

Kermit was trying to calm her down. "Piggy!" he said, flailing his arms. "You are not being replaced, and you have to quit ramming holes in the walls!"

"Oh, you don't like holes in the walls?" challenged Piggy. "Then let me plug them up for you!"

Piggy swung her chair around and smacked poor Hockney with her cast, sending him hurtling toward the wall at top speed.

THIS WAS NOT IN MY JOB DESCRIPTION.

"What on earth got her so upset?" I whispered to Kermit.

"Well"—Kermit gulped—"it seems Miss Piggy is a little irritated about our newest cast member."

"What new cast member?" I asked.

"Hello, big bwudda!" came a horrifying voice from behind me. It was a voice I heard in my nightmares. A voice from the slimy ooze that bubbles in the heart of man's darkest fears.

Within a fraction of a second, I was out of control and flailing my arms like Kermit. "Are you telling me my sister is our newest cast member?!" I shrieked. "Are you insane?"

Pasquale tried to calm me, saying, "Settle down, dude."

"Settle down?" I bellowed. "I'll show you settled down! Hiiiiiii-yaaaaaaa!"

At last I understood the mystery—and deep personal satisfaction—of Miss Piggy's uncontrollable karate chops.

After I cooled off and apologized to Pasquale, Kermit tried to explain what was happening.

"Danvers, don't let this upset you," he said. "The Muppets have always been willing to try new, bold, untested talent. From movies to middle grade books, from music compilation albums to Broadway, from hula-hooping to traditional Russian folk dancing, we just can't say no."

"Reality TV is just the next logical step for us," finished Kermit.

"Heeza right," said Mondo the Lizard. "Do you a-know what ze ratings were like for my last three reality shows?"

"No," I said.

"They were a-terrible! Ifa thees one isn't a hit, I'ma gonna go bankrupt!"

"It's not the reality-show thing that's got me worried," I whispered to Kermit so that Chloe couldn't hear me. "It's my sister. You just don't know what she's like, especially if she's in a position of power."

Happy Birthday to me!
I shall now weceive gifts in order from weast expensive to most expensive.
Psst! I have it on good authority that all the next kid wants for Chwistmas is tube socks and undies.
Eetha my name goes above the marquee or I walk. If you know some wun who can play a sun flower on such short notice, have at it!
Miss Webber's class presents Kindergarten Spring Show
Show time in 10 minutes!

Kermit patted me on the shoulder and said, "Danvers, I'm sure you're just overreacting. Your sister is a charming bundle of natural talent and pizzazz. She is a true Blickensderfer."

SI! HER DISTURBING CUTENESS IS SURPASSED ONLY BY HER NAUSEATING ADORABLENESS, OKAY.

I reluctantly gave in. "Well, I guess a reality show might be interesting, but consider yourself warned."

"Thanks," Kermit said, smiling. "Now if we can just get Piggy to be as understanding as you are."

Piggy went "Hmph!" and rammed her fortified foot into Gonzo's crate of bedbugs.

Boomerang Trout
YAHOO! FALL IN, SQUADRON! THIS PLACE IS NOTHING BUT FELT, FUR, STUFFING, AND FEATHERS. IT'S A WALKIN', TALKIN', ALL-YOU-CAN-EAT BUFFET!

Kermit and Gonzo tried madly to wrangle the bugs back into their crate, but it was too late.

"Gonzo!" Kermit cried. "Now we've got an infestation on our hands!"

"Sorry, Kermit," said Gonzo. "I guess I should have stuck with earwigs!"

All of a sudden, Janice leaned in with a telephone.

DR. HONEYDEW!

I grabbed the phone and said, "Hello?"

Oh, Danvers! I am pleased to announce I've made a breakthrough in solving the mystery of your muppet morphosis. Meet us at your apartment at once!
Beaker, will you please turn down that rap music? Can't you see I'm trying to drive, talk on the phone, and eat a chili dog at the same time?
©DB

CHAPTER 7

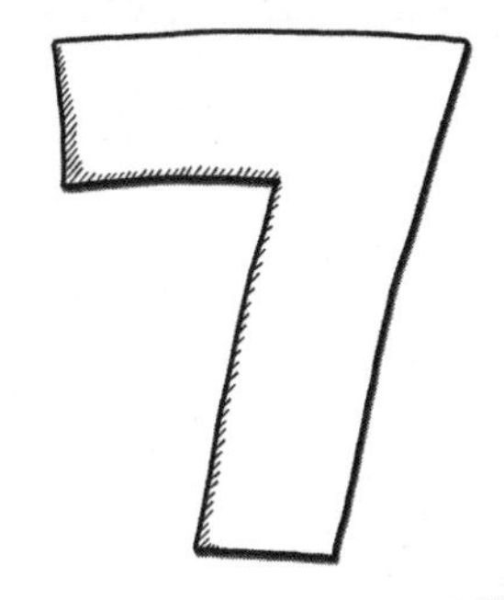

UNPOPULAR SCIENCE
DEC. 11
SCIENTIST OF THE YEAR
DR. BUNSEN HONEYDEW
PLUTONIUM
DANGER!
THE DEJA PEW 5000
SMELL IT AGAIN... FOR THE FIRST TIME.
DR. HONEYDEW'S GREATEST INVENTIONS
VOL. 2
meep!
INSTA-BEARD FORMULA
meep!
DA DA!
TEE HEE!
Alligator egg incubator boxer shorts
meep!
HUMAN HAMSTER BALL
meep.
DO-IT-YOURSELF LASER EYE SURGERY
©DB

Dr. Bunsen Honeydew and Beaker met us in front of my apartment in their tricked-out Muppet Labs van. It looked like an ice-cream truck, except it was full of radioactive fungus spores and atom splitters instead of tasty Dream Pops.

My mom was a little nervous about the situation.

NORMALLY, WE DON'T ALLOW DANVERS TO HAVE UNORTHODOX SCIENTISTS COME OVER WITH DANGEROUS RADIOACTIVE EQUIPMENT AFTER 6 PM.
MUPPET LABS
RACING TEAM
DANGER!
HUNEDU

I managed to sweet-talk my mom into it by telling her how this could solve the mystery of why I was a Muppet. To be honest, I really did want to get back to being my old self. It's cool being a Muppet and all, but sometimes it's not all it's cracked up to be.

What's not so Great about being a Muppet
by Danvers Blickensderfer
Grape Juice
① Drinking grape juice can leave stubborn stains on felty skin.*
* luckily, a little Spray 'N' SLOSH will get it right out.
② Often mistaken for carnival prizes.
Dart Game
Hit the target, win a prize!
Daddy, I want that one with the yellow hair and pink nose!
Just keep walking.
③ Uncontrollable snappy jokes can get you in trouble.
I call it twice-baked meat loaf.
wow! You baked it twice and still didn't get it right.

I have to admit, I was a little worried about going back to my old self. Ever since that green flash, the whole world had become a little fuzzy, not just me. Kermit's theater had popped up right in the heart of Block City, Sam Eagle was running a fine-arts training academy, Rowlf had his own veterinarian hospital.... It was like there had been a disruption in the Space-Time Condominium! If I transformed back, would everything return to its normal old boring ways? Would the Muppets even know who I am? Would Gonzo still want me as his assistant?

It was a risk I had to take.

"So, this is where it all happened," said Dr. Bunsen Honeydew as he walked through my bedroom. "The Muppetmorphosis."

"Meep!" said Beaker, the Muppet Labs' most dedicated—and only—lab assistant, as he scanned the room with a beepy, shiny, computery contraption that looked like a TV remote wearing a space helmet.

Pasquale was with me for moral support, and Curtis was shivering in fear on my shoulder. He had been

a little freaked out by computery bleepy things ever since the last one turned him into Ratzilla.

Beaker pointed his device at the closet on the far side of the room and it started to beep faster and louder, like a metal detector scanning a beach full of bottle caps.

Pasquale pulled out his pocket flashlight and shined it at the closet door as we moved toward it. Beaker's detector started to vibrate all over the place, like it was loaded with jumping beans.

I couldn't take the suspense. "What's it doing?"

"Shhhhhhhhh!" shushed Dr. Honeydew. "The Bleepinator 500Sx has picked up on a mysterious magnetic surge emanating from behind that door. We must approach with extreme caution, as we are dealing with a dangerous, powerful force that could rearrange our molecular matter in a nanosecond. Beaker, you go first."

"Meep?"

Beaker slowly opened the door, and we all clutched one another in terror as we saw a pink blanket pulsating as if something were writhing beneath it. A weird, muffled goo goo *ga ga* sound was coming from it. Beaker reached in cautiously and lifted the blanket, only to find ...

Dr. Honeydew shrieked and fired off his portable electro-gamma zapper, hitting the closet with a crazy blue bolt of electricity, singeing Beaker's hair and vaporizing half of my winter clothes!

"Uh," I said, "I think you just destroyed my sister's Burpy Baby Flufffleberry doll."

"But it fired something at us," said Pasquale.

"Burpy Baby Flufffleberry is equipped with quick-fire baby-spittle action, extra ammo for rapid reload, and a barf radius of five feet," I explained. (Don't ask me how I know this.)

"Extraordinary," said Dr. Honeydew. "What will science come up with next?"

"It better come up with $69.99 to get Chloe a new one, or we're all in hot water," I said.

"Just what are you looking for with that equipment, anyway?" asked Pasquale.

"Well, to be precise…we have no earthly idea," said Dr. Honeydew. "But what we do know is that something in this apartment caused the transformation, and I believe I have devised an ingenious way to find out what."

I felt the cold chrome nose. "Wow! That's some schnoz! What does it do?"

Dr. Honeydew plugged in the Deja Pew 5000 and it started to hum like an old refrigerator. "A recent probe into nasal research discovered that the nose can retain scents and aromas from the past. Some say one healthy honker can contain more than five thousand different smells."

"Kinda like our school locker room," said Pasquale.

"Precisely," continued Dr. Honeydew. "It is quite similar to the way the human brain has the ability to retain something, like a memory or math knowledge."

"I don't think my brain has that feature," I said.

"Oh, don't be silly, young man. Every brain does. The Deja Pew 5000 can go into your nose and pull out exactly what you were smelling according to the date I enter into this computer panel. Here, allow me to demonstrate on Beaker."

Dr. Honeydew reached over and plucked Beaker's nose off his face like a cherry tomato.

FIRST, I WILL INSERT THE SUBJECT'S PROBOSCIS INTO THE MACHINE.
SPLOINK!
MEEEEEEP!

Dr. Honeydew connected some electrode wires to Beaker's head. "And now I will enter a date into the computer—say, August 12, 1996—and then I will activate the Deja Pew. Stand back!"

The machine started to shake and make whirring sounds. Green lights flashed. Beaker herked and jerked. Dreamy flashback harp music filled the air. Suddenly, an image appeared on the television screen that was built into the machine.

It was Beaker, sitting in a field of poppies, his hair blowing gently in the breeze. He looked content.

"You are relaxed, aren't you, Beaker?" said Dr. Honeydew in a soothing voice. "We have gone back to the day you visited that field of flowers outside the city of Charlotte. The aromas in the air were wonderful, weren't they? Poppies, honeysuckle, freshly cut grass..."

"Mmmmmmmmm." Beaker sighed happily.

"But then something else happened that day, didn't it, Beaker?" said Dr. Honeydew, and Beaker started to squirm. On the TV screen, black shadows zipped past Beaker in the flower field, and he began to tremble. Then he sniffed the air.

"Meep!" He shivered.

"You're feeling anxiety now, aren't you, Beaker? You smell something foul. That's because August 12, 1996, was the day of the great North Carolina skunk invasion!"

It was terrifying! Beaker thrashed and screamed. Pasquale covered his eyes. Curtis hid in an empty Cheezy-Q bag.

Dr. Honeydew shut down the machine and patted the trembling Beaker on the back, saying, "It's okay. It was just a memory, my friend." Then the doctor turned to us. "Quick, reach into the right nostril of the Deja Pew and hand me what's inside."

I did as he said and stuck my arm inside the nostril—where I found a glass canister about as big as a thermos. I removed it and handed it to Dr. Honeydew.

Unscrewing the lid from the canister, he held it out for us to sniff. "Tell me what you smell."

Pasquale and I took a whiff. "Holy Toledo! It smells like skunk!"

"Correct!" said Dr. Honeydew. "We just plucked a smell from Beaker's nasal memory. Now, if we can determine what your nose was smelling on the night of your Muppetmorphosis, it could be the first step in undoing your transformation!"

IT WON'T BE EASY. ONCE THIS NOSE IS RUNNING, WE'LL HAVE TO DIG DEEP, AND THERE'S A CHANCE WE COULD BLOW IT. WHAT DO YOU SAY, YOUNG SCIENCE PIONEERS? ARE YOU READY?
AND NOW, A WORD FROM OUR SPONSORS...
SINUS UP, DOC!

CHAPTER

Next week on HOARDING WITH THE STARS
SMELL CANISTER
I STILL CAN'T GET USED TO THE SANS SCHNOZ LOOK.

When I was all wired up and ready, Dr. Honeydew announced, “Before we scientifically investigate the night of your transformation, I would like to enter a series of random dates as a warm-up to the big event. Are you ready?”

“Ready, Doc!” I answered.

BEAKER, SET THE DEJA PEW FOUR YEARS AHEAD!
NOW I SMELL POPCORN. HEY, THIS IS WHEN I MET PASQUALE FOR THE FIRST TIME! WE WERE SEEING OUR FIRST MUPPET MOVIE.
HI. MY NAME'S PASQUALE.
I'M DANVERS. HAVE YOU EVER BEEN FIRED OUT OF A CATAPULT?
AND NOW, IT SMELLS LIKE SAWDUST AND PET FOOD—AWWW! THIS IS WHEN I GOT CURTIS FOR CHRISTMAS! HE WAS JUST A BABY.
HEY, LITTLE GUY!
LOOK AT YOU, CURTIS. YOU'RE SO CUTE!
DEJA PEW 5000

NOW WE WILL SKIP FURTHER AHEAD.
NOW I SMELL BURNT HAIR. OOPS! THIS IS ONE OF OUR EMO SHUN STUNTS GONE WRONG.
I DON'T THINK WE WANT YOU IN THE GROUP ANY-MORE. IT'S TOO DANGEROUS!
I DON'T NEED YOUR GROUP, ANYWAY! I LAUGH AT DANGER! MWA HA HA!
HEY! I SMELL BIRTHDAY CAKE AND PUNCH. THIS WAS CHLOE'S BIRTHDAY PARTY, THE DAY BEFORE I CHANGED.
MAKE A WISH!
SLOW DOWN, DOC! THAT PART WAS RIGHT BEFORE MY TRANSFORMATION!

HERE WE ARE: OCTOBER 4 OF THIS YEAR. PAY ATTENTION FOR A BRIGHT . . .
DEJA PEN 5000
GREEN FLASH!
RUUUUN!
DEJA PEN 5000

The Deja Pew 5000 shook violently and an alarm went off. Smoke poured out of the unit, and the video screen went staticky, then black.

"Meep!" Beaker shouted as he hosed the machine down with a fire extinguisher.

I managed to save my sniffer from the smoldering machine and reattached it to my face.

DO NOT DISTURB!
DAREDEVIL
AT
WORK!
KNOCK! KNOCK!
IS EVERYTHING OKAY IN THERE? I HEARD RUMBLING, ALARMS, SCREAMS, AND EXPLOSIONS.

"It's okay, Mom!" I hollered back. "We were just playing a game of Duck, Duck, Goose that got out of hand!"

"Alas, it was too much for the Deja Pew," said Dr. Honeydew with a sigh. "At least we recorded it all on this disk—Wait just a minute!" He pulled the collection canister out of the nostril and held it up. "It seems we managed to get a sample just before the machine shut down! It's small, but certainly nothing to sneeze at."

A green gas was floating around in the canister. "So that's the last thing I smelled before the big change?" I asked. "Pasquale, come take a look at this."

But Pasquale was too busy tapping away at something on his smart phone. "Uh, oops," he said, looking up at me. "Sorry, I was playing that angry Gonzo chicken game again. I'm so hooked, it's ridiculous."

I dragged him away from his game, and Dr. Honeydew opened the capsule. We all caught a whiff of the green gas and exclaimed, "Green apples and burnt pistachios!"

Actually, Beaker just exclaimed, "Meep!"

"What could it mean, Doc?" I asked.

"There is one gas in the bowels of recorded history that does indeed smell like green apples and burnt pistachios." He pulled out the definitive text on this matter—*The Muppet Labs Big Book of Gases*—and pointed at a chart inside.

"I would like to commence drilling on these premises at once," continued Dr. Honeydew.

"I'll have to ask my parents first." I was gonna have a heck of a time getting my folks to agree to this. They wouldn't even let me drink cranberry juice over Mom's new carpet!

"Don't worry," said Dr. Honeydew. "Beaker is explaining it to them as we speak."

CHAPTER 9

FASCINATING. I'D LIKE TO TAKE A SAMPLE OF THIS MEAT LOAF BACK TO MY LAB FOR FURTHER ANALYSIS.

The next day at school, I was exhausted from my trip down memory nostril. But for some reason, I also felt jazzed. Smelling my life flash right before my schnoz had energized me.

At the beginning of lunch period, I spotted Pasquale and Kip sculpting the cafeteria potato salad into circus animals. (Trust me, it was the only safe thing we could do with our school's cuisine.)

I felt bad. "Of course your hair is ridiculous… ridiculously awesome, that is!" I patted Kip on the back. "Look, Kip. I was a jerk yesterday. A lot has happened since I insulted your 'do. I've seen and smelled things you could only dream of."

"Dude, you're starting to make me feel uncomfortable."

"Don't feel uncomfortable," I said, pulling a big poster out of my backpack. "You should feel like a superstar. Because you are now a member of the boy-band supergroup called 'Mon Emo Shun Swoon,' or M.E.S.S. for short. I've already hung twenty of these suckers!"

"I thought you didn't want to be in a group with me," snapped Kip. "I thought our history was too 'turbocharged.'"

"It was *turbulent*, actually. But I've realized that

I am no peach to deal with sometimes. Not even an overripe kumquat, in fact. I want to make up for it. Let's hang these posters everywhere. Let's put our past aside. Let's record the greatest collaboration since ranch dressing met pizza crust. Whaddya say?"

Pasquale read the poster and flipped. "Download it this Thursday at midnight? Uh...shouldn't you write it, record it, and run it through the automatic voice tuner first?"

"Easy as pie!" I said. "We can whip this sucker out in ten minutes!"

"Yeah," declared Kip. "You forget, you are dealing with not one but two master songwriters here. It'll be a breeze, yo!"

THIRTY MINUTES LATER, YO.

The songwriting wasn't going as well as I had hoped. Lunch was almost over, and all I had written down was "Girl, yo..."

"You know, instead of playing video games, you could be helping us write," I snapped at Pasquale.

"Sorry," he replied. "I can't get past the level with the hurling pies. This game should be outlawed, it's so addictive."

"Lunch period's over in ten minutes. We gotta get crackin'!" I smacked the table.

Kip bolted awake. "Wha? Dude! Wha? Ten minutes? It's time for my daily acoustic set."

"You're gonna sing now?" I asked.

"Yeah, dude. The girls love it when I fiddle around on the guitar and breathe heavily. And hey, I tell you what: I'll announce our upcoming single while I'm at it."

"Good call," I said as Kip grabbed his guitar and got up on the table.

The girls in the lunchroom immediately swooned in unison as Kip announced, "Dudes and dudettes, I'm sure you've seen the exciting posters hanging all over school featuring me and my pal Danvers. Download our new single this Thursday at midnight."

Everyone looked over at Phips and started laughing. He had a big bowl over his head that strangely resembled Kip's slick hairdo.

"Thank you, dudes and dudages," Phips snarked in a cool-cat voice. "It's a little hot in here. A little bit humid. Wanna know why? Cuz there's a new boy

band in town. A supergroup. We're called Motion Slickness. You might have heard our top-ten hit, 'Blinded by My Bangs.'"

The laughter in the cafeteria got louder and louder.

Phips put one hand on his hip and struck a suave pose. "My name's Phips. That's right. Why settle for a Kip when you can have a whole bag of Phips?"

"*Quelle insulte!*" cried Danny Enfant.

Kip slunk down in his seat beside me. "Dude. This is the uncoolest thing in the history of uncoolness."

But everyone in the cafeteria was eating it up and laughing like hyenas.

"Don't let him get to you," I said, trying to keep from giggling. I had to admit, he had Kip down pretty good.

The crowd went nuts as Phips put the shaggy end of a mop on his head, slapped a red radish on his face like a clown nose, and drew pupils on his glasses.

HEY-OOOOOO, EVERYBODY! HEY, WHY DID FOZZIE BEAR CROSS THE ROAD? CUZ THE SIGN SAID *WALKA! WALKA!*

The lunchroom exploded in claps and cheers.

"Sorry, folks!" he said, laughing. "I know that joke was un*bear*able!"

Now he had done it. Phips had stepped on the wrong Muppet!

"*Sacre bleu!*" Danny steamed.

"It's a good thing I'm, like, into yoga and whole grains," Kip said calmly, "because otherwise, I might not be able to control my rage."

Pasquale tried to calm us down. "Don't let him get to you. That's what he wants. Just remember, today after school at the Muppet Theater, we will record the greatest hit single since 'Who Let the Pygmy Shrews Out?' and this joker will be yesterday's news. Isn't that right, Danvers? Danvers?"

My anger was flowing over. "That kid must be stopped," I said, smoldering. "Whatever it takes, that kid must be stopped."

HEY, DANVERT*IBLE*, WE'RE COOL, RIGHT? YOU KNOW I LOVE YOU.

CHAPTER 10

After school, Pasquale and I headed back to our internships, and we brought all the members of Emo Shun with us. The Muppet Theater was utter chaos that day. (Hey, did you ever notice that "chaos" and "Chloe" start with the same two letters?)

Not only was the place crawling with bedbugs, but the battle of the divas had really started cookin'. Piggy was having a code-red meltdown, wheeling around the studio with her battle-ram leg. Chloe was just standing by, smiling real cute-like, while Rizzo and Mondo were getting it all on video.

"*Moi* has had it!" Piggy bellowed. "I will not tolerate any more insults from this immature ingenue!"

Kermit tried to calm Piggy. "What did Chloe do to get you this upset?"

ALL I DID WAS BWING MISS PIGGY A GWASS OF MILK, BECAUSE AT HER ADVANCED AGE, SHE NEEDS ALL THE CALCIUM SHE CAN GET SO HER LEG WILL GET ALL BETTA.

Best of the Muppet Theater's DIVA Showdown moments (vol. 1 of 35)

Hmmph! I didn't realize we were running a daycare.

I thought this was an old folks' home.

my Gwamma wuved your act as a young girl.

Dressing room

MISS PIGGY

Don't worry. I'm not here to weplace you, but you might want to have this doorknob lowered just in case.

It's santa calling. He's looking for someone to play an elf!

“Piggy,” said Kermit. “Chloe was just trying to be helpful.”

“Mmmm-hmmmmm!” Piggy hmphed, then turned to Chloe. “And why don’t you tell Kermit how you stole my advertising gig?!”

“My mommy taught me dat stealing is wong, espeshwy fwum an actwess of your stature.”

“Why, you!” Piggly howled, lunging for my sister. Sweetums had to hold Piggy back.

Kermit was getting flustered. “Can anyone tell me what happened?”

“Sure,” said Hockney. “You see, Miss Piggy was scheduled to do her glamorous photo shoot for DeBoot Footwear on soundstage 3D. When the photographer noticed that her leg was in a cast, he almost canceled the shoot. But luckily—I mean, unfortunately—Chloe happened to walk in and do an impromptu song and dance in her DeBoot deluxe cowboy boots. So…she filled in for Miss Piggy.”

Kermit tried to console Piggy. “Look, Chloe did you a favor. Besides, there is no way you can shoot a commercial for footwear until that cast comes off.”

"ROOTIN' TOOTIN' COWBOY BOOTIN'!"
AND EVEN WHEN IT DOES COME OFF, OKAY, WHO WANTS TO BUY THE SHOES FROM A PIG, OKAY?
OKAY, PEPE! YOU'RE NOT HELPING!
DeBooT
A FEET OF ACCOMPLISHMENT
DeBooT

FUMIGATING IN HER
DRESSING ROOM?
EVACUATE IMMEDIATELY!

"Well, it's obvious that *moi* is not needed!" Piggy announced, wheeling away. "If anyone wants me, I'll be fuming in my dressing room! *Au revoir!*"

"Man, that sister of yours has a way of getting under people's skin," said Pasquale.

"She has a permanent residence under mine," I said with a sigh.

I didn't mind that Piggy and my sister were fighting. The distraction gave me time to finish writing our new song and set up the recording studio. It was Kip, Danny, and Cody's first time at the theater, and they were signing some legal paperwork involving the complicated merger of our two boy bands.

SIGN PAPER!
SIGN PAPER!
VØØRNA STÜKELELE FÎRDEE FLINGENSTØØFERDEE BØØDLE, YØØBETCHA!
COULD YOU REPEAT THAT LAST PART?
RELEASE FORM

By 4:30, everyone was ready to start, and Kermit walked up to his podium.

"Hi, ho, everybody! It's so good to have Danvers's friends joining us today for a true collaboration of talent. I really think this new song will explode off the charts."

"*Si*, like a huge bomb, okay," said Pepe.

We slapped on our headphones as Kermit said, "Okay, is everybody ready?"

Kermit turned to Pasquale, who was at the soundboard, and said, "Sound engineer, how are our levels?"

But Pasquale didn't answer. He was tapping away at something.

"Pasquale!" I yelled. "You better not be playing that Gonzo chicken game again!"

He looked up, embarrassed. "Sorry! I'm about to beat the level with the angry puffins." I rolled my eyes. That blasted game was starting to take over my best friend.

"All right!" Kermit announced, tapping his foot. "One, two...One, two, three and..."

GIRL, don't Be Rash
by Danvers Blickensderfer and Kip Strummer
My baby took me hiking, yo
Soon my heart was breakin', yo
This rash I can't be fakin', yo
Got me some poison Ivy toe.
Gotta tell that gal 'o mine
I need some Calamine
'bout to go out of my mind
Itchy Poison Ivy vines.
Girl, don't be rash
Girl, don't be cruel
If I don't cure this fast
Gonna miss some school.
Itchy Itchy Itchy, Yo
Scratchy Scratchy Scratchy, yo
Itchy Itchy Itch
Poison Sumac
Daddy
Calamine lotion
itch relief
great on Salads!
AND NOW I, THE GREAT GONZO, WILL ATTEMPT TO LEAP THIRTY FLAMING HOT-DOG CARTS WEARING A PAIR OF YODELING PERUVIAN CATFISH!
©DB

"Gonzo!" Kermit shouted, flailing his arms. "We're just recording the song. You don't have to do the stunt! Save that for the live performance!"

"Just the song?" Gonzo gasped. "I'd better extinguish those flaming hot-dog carts!" He grabbed the nearest fire extinguisher and darted off.

It took us a couple of takes to get the perfect performance, but it was worth it.

"Okay, Pasquale," I said, handing him the master tape. "You have until Thursday night at midnight to get this thing mastered and posted online. So lay off that birdbrained video game!"

"Don't worry," said Pasquale. "I'll have it done lickety-chicken, I mean chickadee-split, I mean lickety-split!"

Pepe suddenly came through the door, looking extra suave in a leather jacket. "Step away from my clients, okay. If you want to speak to them, you have to speak into me! I am going to make them huge stars! I am their new publicizer."

"I think you mean publicist," I said. "And I don't remember any of us hiring you."

OF COURSE YOU HIRE ME. IT'S RIGHT HERE ON PAGE 108, OKAY.
BUT WE'RE ONLY ON PAGE 100!
DON'T BORE ME WITH THE MINOR DETAILS, OKAY.

Kip pulled me aside, saying, "Maybe he's right, dude. We could use some representation."

"Hmmm," I said, turning to Pepe. "First, I wanna see your so-called plan for making us *huge stars*."

Pepe unfolded some ratty-looking paper. "But of course. I have a detailed action plan for stardom, okay. Don't mind the grease stains, okay—I write it on an old napkin at the doughnut shop this morning."

Pepe's Action packed Super Stardom plan for success, okay

illustrated by Danvers Blickensderfer

"I'll have to think about it," I told Pepe as everyone started to pack up for the day.

That's when I spotted Fozzie Bear on his way out. "Hey, Fozzie!" I called. "I've been meaning to talk to you."

Fozzie perked up. "And I've been meaning to listen to you! Wocka! Wocka!"

I WAS WONDERING... YOU SEE, I NEED SOME ADVICE FROM A MASTER COMEDIAN. A GIANT IN THE INDUSTRY. A COMIC LEGEND. SOMEONE RESPECTED BY HIS PEERS...
YESSSS?
DO YOU KNOW ANYONE LIKE THAT?

I told Fozzie I was just pulling his leg. He looked down at his leg and said, "Wow. I didn't feel a thing." I explained that this was a figure of speech, then proceeded to tell him all about the nightmare new kid, Phips Terlington, and how he was making me crazy. "I don't know what to do about this guy. He's making me and Kip the butt of all his jokes, and I don't wanna be the butt of anything!"

"You should challenge him to an old-fashioned joke showdown," said Fozzie. "Just like comedians did in the Old West."

"But where?" I asked.

"Anywhere!" said Fozzie. "The lunchroom, the playground, General Chow's Sweet and Sour Donut Emporium... They have the best ravioli in town, by the way."

Kermit was walking by, and stopped to join our conversation. "It's true," he said, backing Fozzie up. "A joke showdown is a time-honored tradition in show business. One of my uncles back in the swamp used to hold an impromptu comedy competition every Friday at the Silly Pad Club. He called it the Frog Jam."

HAVE YOU EVER SEEN A FROG JAM?
NO, BUT I'VE SEEN A JELLY FISH, AN ALLIGATOR HIDE, AND AN APPLE GET SAUCY ON A NATURE PRESERVE!
FER SURE!

"A comedy jam. That's a good idea," I said.

"I could make this happen, okay," said Pepe. "For fifty percent of the profits, of course."

"All right, Pepe," said Kermit. "By the way, it's a free event."

"And fifty percent of free is...Oh! *Dios mío!* I'm broke!"

I was starting to warm up to this idea. I couldn't resist a good throwdown at a showdown. "We'll have to find the perfect venue," I said.

"We could do it here, at the Muppet Theater," Fozzie suggested. "All we need are some impartial judges."

WE CAN DO IT! WE'RE IMPARTIAL.
I HAVE IMPARTIAL HEARING IN MY LEFT EAR!

"No way! I don't want you guys judging me," I said, shaking my head. "You'll tear me apart."

Fozzie, surprisingly, jumped to their defense. "Actually, if it weren't for Statler and Waldorf, I wouldn't be the comedian I am today."

"Don't blame us, bear!" said Waldorf.

Kermit looked iffy on this. "I don't know, Gonzo. We're already having enough trouble with the escaped bedbugs. They ate all the hay in Camilla's chicken coop."

"Don't worry, folks!" shouted Kermit. "I have pest control coming in tomorrow."

Rizzo and his film crew popped in.

"You know," said Rizzo, focusing his camera on me, "this comedy-jam thingy sounds like a great TV opportunity. Maybe Chloe could open the show with a big musical number."

Pepe immediately jumped in with disapproval. "I don't know if I want her stealing the spotted lights from my clients, okay."

"I really don't care what she does anymore." I shrugged. "And I haven't even hired you as our *publicizer* yet."

"It's publicist, okay," Pepe said.

Kermit perked up. "I think it's a great idea, Rizzo. And it would make a really exciting finale for your reality show."

WHY DON'T YOU JUST GIVE HER MY PARKING SPACE WHILE YOU'RE AT IT? I'M SURE SHE NEEDS A PLACE TO PARK HER TRICYCLE!!!
DRESSING ROOM

While Kermit went over to console and defuse Miss Piggy, I turned to Rizzo. "This is great!" I said. "We can do this comedy showdown, and everyone will see that I am way funnier than Phips. We'll see who's left standing as champ class clown!" Rizzo turned his camera off and pulled me aside.

"Hey, kid," he whispered. "If you really wanna get to this Phips kid, you might have to take the gloves off, if you know what I mean."

"But I don't wear gloves. They cause chafing."

"I mean you might have to dig up some dirt on this kid. Maybe he still sleeps with a Huggy Wuggy Bear. Maybe he runs a stolen Italian sports-car crime ring. Maybe he puts hot sauce in his ears and knits baby booties!"

WHAT'S SO STRANGE ABOUT THAT, OKAY?

"All I'm saying is, if you find out something embarrassing from his past, then you could, say, accidentally mention it in front of a couple hundred kids. It'll give you the leg up when it comes time for your comedy showdown. That kid'll be a nervous wreck. You'll shake his confidence and steamroll right over him at the big event."

I couldn't believe my ears. "Rizzo! I wouldn't sink that low, ever."

Or *would* I?

OKAY, WE'VE THOUGHT IT OVER AND DECIDED THAT WE WILL HIRE YOU AS OUR PUBLICIST AFTER ALL.
THAT IS SO EIGHT PAGES AGO, OKAY.

CHAPTER 11

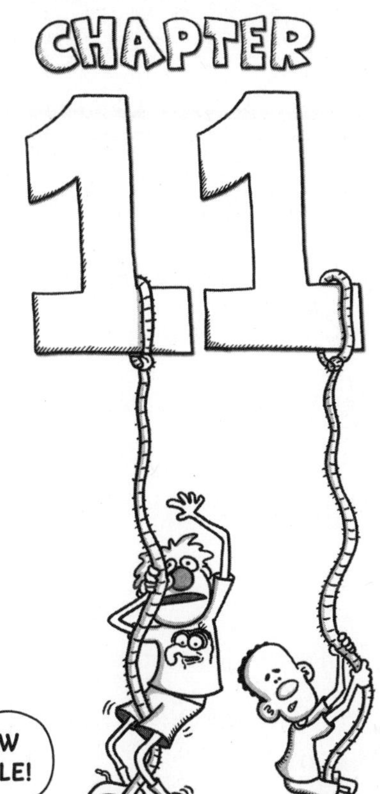

The next day at school, Pasquale looked like he hadn't slept in four days. The bags under his eyes were as dark as licorice sticks, and he had the energy of an elderly tree sloth.

I THINK I MIGHT HAVE TO GO HOME SICK.

"Pasquale, you're a wreck," I said. "You must have been working all night on our new single."

"Actually, um, I haven't even touched it." Pasquale moaned. "I'm on level three hundred on that stupid game."

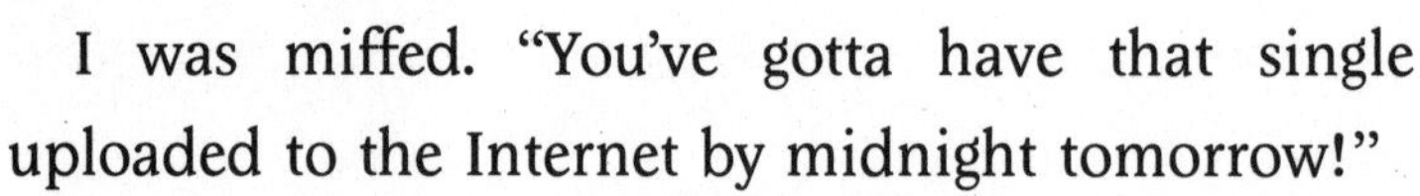

I was miffed. "You've gotta have that single uploaded to the Internet by midnight tomorrow!"

"Don't worry, I will. If I could just take it easy and relax for a bit, I'd be all right."

Unfortunately for Pasquale, our next class was P.E. with Coach Kraft, whose idea of relaxation was crushing steel ball bearings with his teeth.

As we got suited up in our stinky gym clothes, Kip came up and laid some interesting info on us.

"Dude," he whispered, "I just overheard the principal talking to Phips."

"Yeah?" I said.

"He said he needed Phips's records from the last three schools he attended since fifth grade. Three schools in one year, yo."

"Whoa. I bet he got kicked out of each school for his delinquent behavior," I said. "You know, all those pranks, bad jokes, and tomato-throwing."

"Yeah," snarked Pasquale. "Nothing will get you expelled faster than lobbing soft vegetables."

"I'm not kidding. This is good ammunition," I said, rubbing my hands together like a master villain. "We can use this to bring that kid down."

Pasquale didn't approve. "I say, let it go. This isn't our style."

Suddenly, I felt a warm wind on the top of my head, like the hot breath of an enraged moose.

You don't mess with Coach Kraft. Even his earlobes have muscles. Seriously, he works out for, like, five hours a day.

The Coach Kraft Workout Plan:
So You can look so ripped that your muscles get that creepy bulging vein look
1. Wake up and immediately power lift 500 pounds.
Oh yeah! feel the burn!
2. Breakfast- smoothie made from 23 raw eggs, dry ice, and an adobe brick.
Brick
Oh yeah! Just to give it a little crunch.
3. Short break to watch Baby Einstein.
OOOH! It's my favorite episode with the Choo Choo train!
4. Pull car to work with teeth.
Ooooh yeah! much more gas efficient!
©Danvers Blickensderfer

Coach made the whole class line up on the soccer field like soldiers, then grunted, "I understand we got us a new student, named Mr. Pipps."

"Actually, it's Phips," said Phips.

Coach Kraft got up in Phips's face. "You correctin' me, boy? I don't like to be disrespected!"

"I didn't mean to be disrespect*able*, Coach," said Phips. "I've got nothing against you. I especially enjoyed your performance in *Cronar: The Barbarian.*"

Some of the class snickered, while most of us got deadly silent.

I was afraid Coach was about to explode like an overheated coffeepot, but he relaxed, stopped shaking, and said, "We got a jokester here, class. You know what happens to jokesters? They get to run up and down the bleachers twenty-five times carrying a thirty-pound tub of Icy Burn medicated sports cream, which you'll be needin' later, I might add."

If I was going to fight dirty, like Rizzo said, this was my chance. Before I knew what I was doing, I opened my big mouth.

"I'm sure he's used to that kind of punishment, Coach," I announced. "What with him being kicked out of three different schools in the last year and all."

"Oh, no," moaned Pasquale.

The other kids gasped, and Coach growled, "Three different schools in one year? What kind of troublemaker are you, Pips?"

Phips looked down and said, "Yep. It's lament*able*. I'm a troublemaker, all right, but I didn't get kicked out of those schools. My dad's in the army, and he keeps getting shipped around to different towns. I hardly even get to know people, and then I have to move again. I was hoping this time it would be different."

The class let out an "Awwwwww."

Button Hauser sniffled at me. "How could you be so heartless?!"

Boy, did I feel like a louse. Actually, more like the invisible parasites that live on the belly of a louse.

Even Coach Kraft got all teary-eyed.

MY DADDY WAS A MILITARY MAN, TOO. IT WAS A HARD LIFE. MY ONLY FRIEND WAS A STUFFED SQUIRREL NAMED SPUTTERS.

What a disaster! Now everyone felt sorry for Phips and thought I was Mayor McJerk of Jerkytown.

Kip walked up and patted me on the back, saying, "That really worked out well, dude."

After class, Pasquale forced me to go up to Phips at his locker and apologize.

"Sorry, Phips," I mumbled.

"No worries," Phips said, shrugging. "It's all good."

Pasquale stepped up and said, "I, for one, was horrified at my friend's baseless accusations."

"I said it's all good, kid!" Phips laughed. "Hey, your name's Pasquabble, right? And you're some kind of math whiz?"

"Uh, it's Pasquale, and yeah, I suppose I'm okay at math," answered Pasquale. "Why?"

"I'm reading this book on the meaning of pi—you know, that symbol with the squiggly lines? I thought you could help me with some questions. Like, what does pi stand for, who discovered it, what flavor is it?"

"What flavor is pi?" asked Pasquale.

That's when Phips pulled a big whipped cream–covered pie out of his locker and smacked Pasquale in the face with it.

"I don't know!" Phips laughed. "You tell me!"

Everyone standing in the hall around us cracked up.

"Geez! Tomatoes. Pies. Does he have a mini-fridge in there or something?" asked Kip.

Seeing my best friend wearing a pie set something off inside me. It was bad enough when Phips picked on me or Kip, but you don't mess with Pasquale.

THIS FRIDAY, PHIPS! COMEDY SHOW-DOWN WITH ME! BE THERE OR BE SQUARED!
GAME ON!

"Of course I'll be there! It is unmiss*able*." Phips laughed, walking off with his chuckling friends. "We're cool, right?"

So it was set. I was gonna have my shot at mopping the floor with this Phips charac— "Wait a minute!" I panicked. "I don't know anything about stand-up comedy!"

Pasquale wiped the whipped cream from his face, pulled a flyer out of his locker, and said, "Relax. I'm way ahead of you."

Sam Eagle teaching a comedy class? Fozzie, sure… but Sam? That guy seemed about as funny as a congressional hearing. It didn't sound right to me…but I was so desperate, I would have taken comedy tips from a carrot.

YOU CALLED?

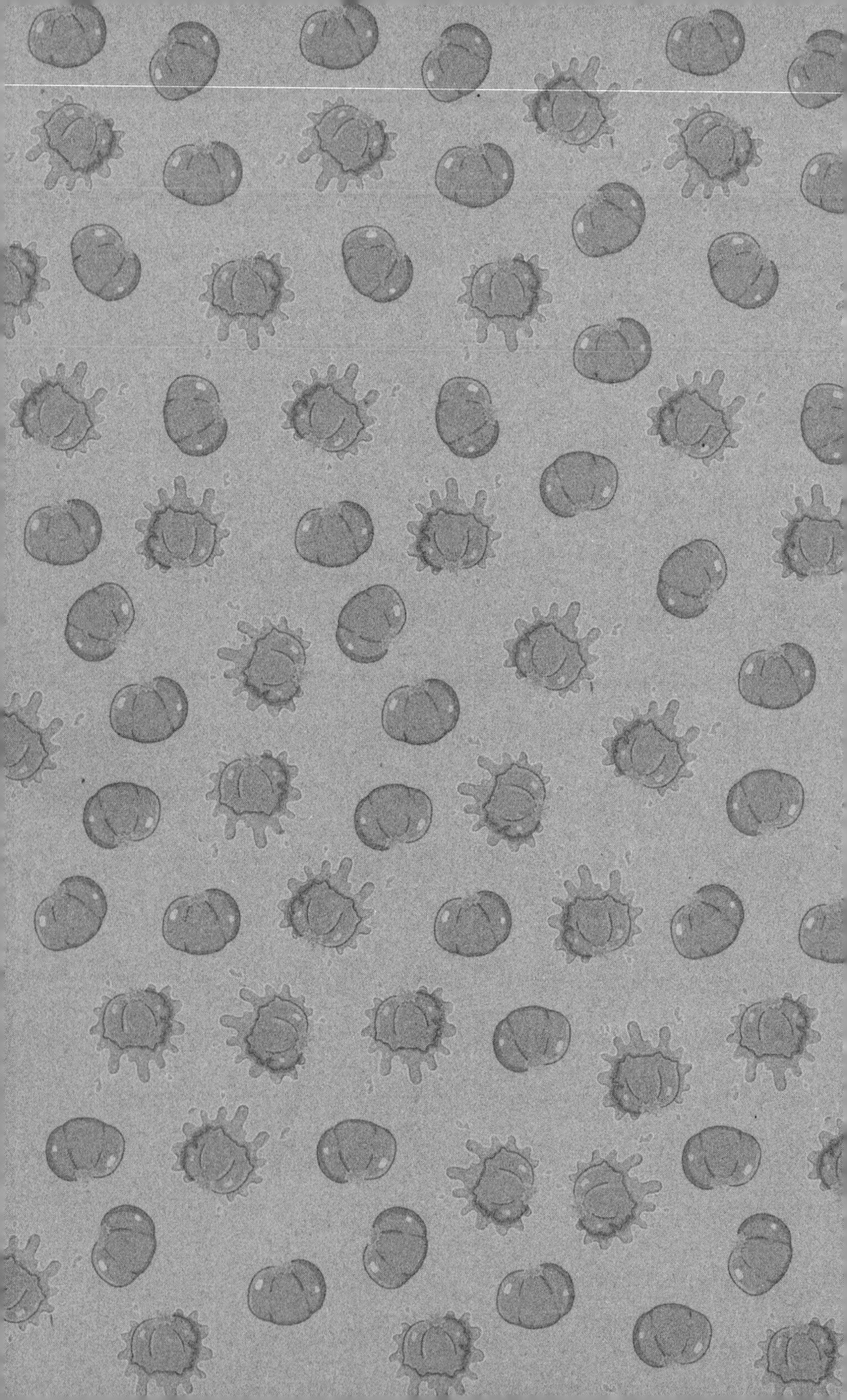

CHAPTER 12

WHY ARE YOU FILMING ME?
BUSTER CHAPBUCKLE
E PLURIBUS UNUM
JUST GETTING SOME PRINCIPAL PHOTOGRAPHY. GET IT? YOU'RE THE PRINCIPAL AND... OH, FORGET IT!

Kermit gave us permission to miss an afternoon of our internships so we could attend Sam's comedy class. Pasquale said he wanted to learn about comedy, too, but I'm pretty sure I know the real reason he wanted to join us. Minette and Ingy were going to be there, and let's just say that underneath that nerdy exterior, Pasquale is a major playa.

YEAH. WE'RE MOVING BEYOND THE BOY-BAND HEARTTHROB STAGE AND DABBLING IN COMEDY. YOU KNOW HOW IT IS IN THIS BUSINESS.

"Ahem!" Sam Eagle coughed from the front of the class. "Good evening, students. As many of you know, Eagle Talon Academy prides itself on developing young minds, then casting them off to spread their wings and fly."

Hmmm...flying brains? I was hooked already.

"For the first time," Sam continued, "we are offering a course specifically rooted in classic, tasteful, family-friendly American comedy."

I raised my hand. "But Principal Eagle, don't most of your graduates end up at the Muppet Theater, where folks waltz with chickens, stuntmen dance with cheese, and Fozzie Bear polkas with a penguin?"

Sam hung his head in shame and slapped his forehead. "Regrettably, yes. That is precisely why I have started this class. I envision a day when my graduates bring their knowledge of classy, old-timey comedy to the Muppet Theater and put a stop to the barrage of cheap, vulgar humor."

WITH MY GUIDANCE, THE STEADY STREAM OF BATHROOM HUMOR WILL SLOW TO A TRICKLE.
E PLURIBUS UNUM

Sam pulled down a screen in the front of the classroom and pointed at a black-and-white picture of a very serious-looking dude in a black hat.

"This, my young, impressionable students, is renowned silent-movie comedy legend Buster Chapbuckle. Everything modern man knows about comedy can be traced to Mr. Chapbuckle and, arguably, the invention of the kazoo."

Sam eagle's Classic, Respectable, decent, All-American Comedy tips

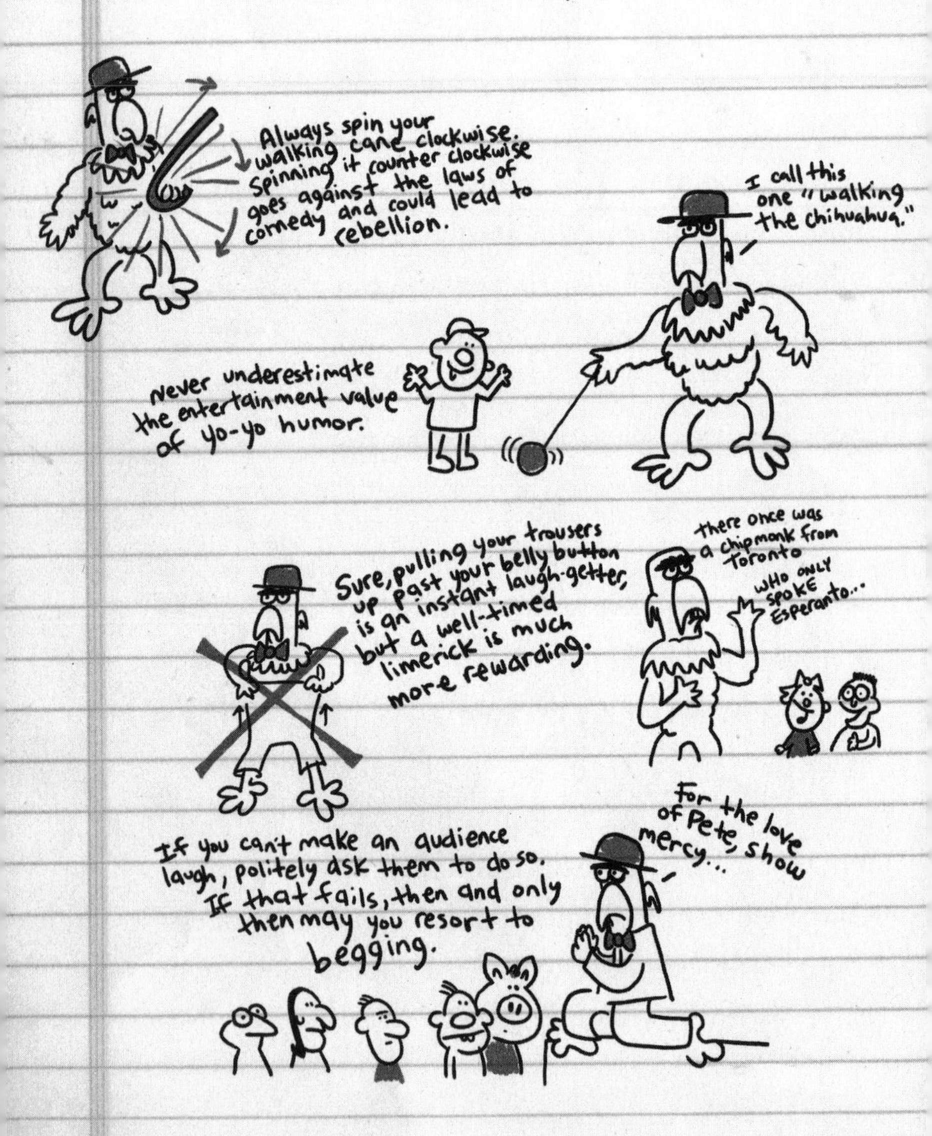

Always spin your walking cane clockwise. Spinning it counter clockwise goes against the laws of comedy and could lead to rebellion.
I call this one "walking the chihuahua."
Never underestimate the entertainment value of yo-yo humor.
Sure, pulling your trousers up past your belly button is an instant laugh-getter, but a well-timed limerick is much more rewarding.
There once was a chipmunk from Toronto
WHO ONLY SPOKE Esperanto...
If you can't make an audience laugh, politely ask them to do so. If that fails, then and only then may you resort to begging.
For the love of Pete, show mercy...

The class had barely started, but I already knew these tips were about as fresh as Gladys the lunch lady's carrot-and-raisin salad.

"Mr. Eagle," I said, raising my hand, "these comedy pointers are very, uh, enlightening, but surely a man of your experience knows some jokes that are a little more, um... edgy?"

"I don't know what you mean." Sam shook his head.

"You know—groundbreaking, out there, controversial."

"Oh, of course." He nodded. "You mean knock-

knock jokes! I have thousands of great knock-knock jokes that I could share—"

Kip stepped in. "I think what Danvers is saying is that beneath that smooth, calm demeanor of yours lurks a true comedy wild man. We just know you've got some killer, outrageous jokes, yo."

Sam looked around, then walked over and locked the door. "Well, I suppose I could teach you Buster Chapbuckle's secret formula for rebel comedy."

The class erupted in cheers.

"But I must warn you," continued Sam. "What I am about to reveal must never be practiced, especially in school. Total anarchy could ensue." Sam brandished a piece of chalk and scribbled his recipe for rambunctious comedy genius on the board.

"He's gotta be kidding," Kip said, sighing.

Sam slammed his fist on the board. "Banana peel plus foot equals comedy! Remember this, students. It is the big bang theory of buffoonery. A banana peel by itself is not funny."

A familiar voice rang out from the back of the class. "But Mr. Eagle, what if the banana peel is doing this?"

AAAARGH!
IT'S THE ABOMINABLE BANANA!

I was furious.

"How'd he get in here?" asked Kip.

"Young man," Sam Eagle snapped at Phips, "comedy class is no place for wisecracks. Sit down."

Sam plopped a huge, old-timey movie projector on his desk. "Now then, I have acquired an extensive collection of hours upon hours of Mr. Chapbuckle's best films, all of which we will watch right now."

"Ugh!" Phips moaned. "Stewardess! Can I get a pillow and a blanket? Zzzzzzz!"

The class roared with laughter. Even Ingy and Minette were chuckling, which really irked Pasquale.

"Oh," moaned Sam. "I should seriously reconsider opening up this course to students who are not enrolled in this fine institution."

Sam flipped off the lights and showed us about five hundred Chapbuckle movies, each of them slightly more exciting than sandpapering a corn cob.

About halfway through hour two hundred of watching Chapbuckle films, I slipped to the back of the class, where Phips was sitting. "Why are you here?" I whispered.

"It said on the flyer that anyone is welcome to come." Phips shrugged. "I need to hone my comedy skills for our big showdown. Now leave me alone. I'm trying to watch some classical cinematical genius at work."

After comedy class, I was grumbly. "I don't think we learned anything."

"I learned Minette's phone number," Pasquale said, smiling.

DUDE. WHY DON'T WE JUST GET SOME COMEDY TIPS FROM YOUR BUDS AT THE MUPPET THEATER? I MEAN, YOU WORK WITH SOME OF THE FUNNIEST CATS IN THE BUSINESS.
I DON'T WORK WITH ANY CATS. I WORK WITH A PIG, AND A FROG, AND A LOT OF CHICKENS, AND A—

"I'm talking about Fozzie—he's a comedian… kind of. And Pepe and Rowlf are funny, too. And I dig those old dudes who are always following you around," said Kip.

"Statler and Waldorf? Are you out of your—" I stopped in mid-sentence. "Hold on! Kip, for once, you have a great idea!"

"Uh…thanks?"

I was jazzed. "We will visit each of the Muppet comedy masters and learn their secrets! Come on, Kip. This is going to be awesome. We can do a two-man show! Two is always better than one!"

Kip stopped me. "Sorry, dude. Comedy showdowns are strictly one on one. Besides, after watching those Chapped Busterknuckle films, I've come to realize that laughs are not my bag. I can't risk bombing on the big stage—I've got my fans and my hair to think about. You'll have to go it alone."

CHAPTER 13

THEY CHUCKLE AT CHALLENGE.
THEY DISS DANGER.
THEY CACKLE AT CONFRONTATION!
THE 5 MASTERS
RATED PGIS
PRETTY GOOD I SUPPOSE

As I approached the temple of the wise and great Master Fozzie, Curtis sat on my shoulder, providing companionship on my quest and annoyingly munching on Cheezy-Qs right in my ear.

Suddenly, I spotted Fozzie from across the room. He was striking the one-footed crane stance.

"There! That's better!" said Fozzie. "So, I hear that you are seeking comedy guidance, young grasshopper."

"How do you know that?" I asked. "You must be able to read minds."

"No," said Fozzie, "but I can read e-mails. Gonzo told me to expect you. Now, the first rule of stand-up comedy is: Never forget your jokes. Memorization is key. It's like that old saying: 'Fool me once, shame on me. Fool me twice, shame on…on…' Oh, how does it go? Aw, never mind—it's not important!"

"Wait!" I said. "Master Fozzie, there is a specific reason I came to you. You see, I need to visit Master Rowlf to learn the art of puns, Statler and Waldorf to learn the craft of the zinger, Master Pepe to understand the ways of wackiness, and…"

YOU NEED ME TO TEACH YOU THE PERFECT JOKE, RIGHT?
ACTUALLY, I NEED A RIDE. I HEAR YOU HAVE A CAR THAT WORKS.
LET ME GET MY KEYS.

Our first stop was Master Rowlf.

"What do you mean, a 'play on words'?" I asked.

"It's like that old song, 'You say beige. I say taupe. Let's call the whole thing off-white.'" said Rowlf.

"I think I get it," said Fozzie. "So, instead of saying, 'I'm going to see a comedian competition in an old shack,' you'd say—"

"I'm going to a sit-down for a stand-up standoff in a lean-to!" I shouted.

The next stop on our quest was to see the old masters Statler and Waldorf. They were perched high above us, shouting bits of wisdom down our way.

"Masters," I said, "I need a lesson in the art of the zinger."

"Can you believe it?" snapped Waldorf. "He thinks we're his teachers!"

"Talk about old school!" said Statler. "Ha ha!"

Before we could go any farther, the old masters demanded $49.99 up front.

"Times are tough, kid," said Statler.

"Yeah," added Waldorf. "Cheap jokes don't come cheap, you know!"

NOW, LESSON NUMBER ONE. TAKE IT FROM A SEASONED, TOUGH OLD BUZZARD: IF SOMEONE GETS SAUCY WITH YOU, IT'S PERFECTLY OKAY TO GIVE THEM A GOOD-NATURED RIBBING.

ALL THIS TALK ABOUT BARBECUE IS MAKING ME HUNGRY!

I wasn't sold on their tactics. "I don't know, old wise ones," I said. "I'm not sure throwing out insults is my style."

Statler swirled his cane at me. "Well," he said, "if you don't throw them, someone else will. You should always be prepared for zingers, because there will definitely be hecklers at your show."

"How do you know that?"

"Because we will definitely be at your show! Ha ha!" said Waldorf.

I was starting to think I just wasn't cut out for comedy.

Statler took my arm and said, "Look, kid, a dame

once told me, 'To make it in comedy, you gotta have thick skin, support yourself, and step on a few toes.'"

"That's right. She called you an *old heel*! Ha ha ha!" added Waldorf.

As I walked away, I felt like I really hadn't learned anything.

Fozzie and I left the two old masters and made our way over the misty mountains.

"Old wise and furry one," I said, "there is one more comedy legend I seek. A strange little master of comedic wit called Pepe."

I turned back and scanned the craggy rocks. Sure enough, I caught a glimpse of two bulging eyes staring at me from behind a dry shrub.

"It's Pepe," I whispered. "I need him to teach me how to be completely comedic."

"Be careful, my son," whimpered Fozzie. "As I once learned at Swedish Chef's all-you-can-eat buffet, shellfish can be unpredictable."

Pepe crawled out from behind the bush and swaggered toward me.

"You wanna throw down, okay?" he said.

"No! I don't wanna fight you!"

"No, no, no. Do you wanna throw down a blanket? I'm having a pick-a-nick, okay. I have some fine aged cheese and the little chicken nuggets shaped like zoo animals, okay."

So we threw down a blanket on the hillside and dined on fine cuisine while Pepe taught us everything he knew about comedy.

WHAT BOOK DO YOU HAVE THERE?
THIS, MY FRIEND, IS THE LATEST CRAZE IN COMEDY, OKAY. IT IS ONE HUNDRED PERCENT LLAMA JOKES.
LLAMA JOKES
ANIMAL NUGGETS

I looked at Pepe like he was crazy. "Llama jokes?"

"That's right. Llamas are all the rage this year, okay. I hear all the major zoos are carrying them."

I was skeptical. "I don't think my audience is going to find those kinds of jokes funny."

"Hey! Save the drama for your llama, okay!" snapped Pepe. "You can find that joke on page thirty-three, by the way."

Fozzie seemed to be into them. "Tell us another one!"

"Okay," said Pepe. "Yo llama is so hairy, people think she is an alpaca, okay! Get it? An alpaca?"

"As in *alpaca* my bags and meet you at the airport? Wocka! Wocka!" Fozzie laughed.

"That's a good one, okay!" Pepe cackled. "I'm going to write that down!"

Then, unfortunately, it was my turn. I had never made a llama joke in my life.

OKAY, I'LL TELL YOU A LLAMA JOKE IF YOU LET ME **PERU**SE YOUR BOOK! GET IT? PERU...BECAUSE THAT'S WHERE LLAMAS COME FROM?
IF YOU CAN'T MAKE THE FUNNY LLAMA JOKE, DON'T EVEN TRY, OKAY. YOU HAVE UPSET CONSUELA HERE, AND SHE MAY SPIT AT YOU, OKAY.

I made one more feeble attempt. "Geez, Consuela," I squeaked, "don't be such a *llama* queen!"

Pepe gave me the look of death. "Oh, boy. Now you have done it, okay. You have insulted all llamas from South America all the way to northern South America, okay."

Consuela definitely looked like she wanted to shower me in freshly chewed cud. "Okay, Master Pepe," I said, nervously shuffling away. "You have been most generous, but we've gotta be going."

I turned to Fozzie. "Let's get out of here!"

We took off running for Fozzie's car.

"Come back, okay!" yelled Pepe, scurrying after us. "Consuela and I were going to demonstrate our chinchilla juggling act! Chinchillas are going to be very big this spring, okay! Mark down my words!"

Fozzie and I finally made it back from our long trek.

He took my hand. "Young grasshopper, you are ready for battle. Your first challenge shall be to call all of the masters together to demonstrate your skills."

"But I still feel unprepared," I said. "Can't I train a little while longer?"

"It is not possible. I've got to get home." Fozzie sighed. "Ma Bear's dropping by for salmon and green-bean casserole, and my place is a *pig*sty."

CHAPTER 14

Well, okay, so maybe my quest for comedy wasn't that exciting, and maybe I found Statler and Waldorf at the top of the Wise Acres Retirement Home instead of Mount Fuji, but all the tips I got did sort of help build my confidence. I wasn't even that mad when Fozzie told everyone to come over for an impromptu practice gig in my living room.

POPPED CORN, OKAY $2.00
I TOLD YOU, I WILL LET YOU HAVE FIVE PERCENT OF THE SALES, OKAY, NOT FIVE PERCENT OF THE POPCORN, OKAY. BAD RODENT!

Even though it was a just a rehearsal, I had severe stage fright.

"Don't be nervous. This is nothing," Fozzie comforted me. "The first time I ever performed was for three hundred other bears at the Third Annual Out of Hibernation Wake-Up Jamboree."

"And they liked your act?"

"Not exactly. That was the moment I first realized that bears may eat their own."

I pulled out some index cards I had made with all my best material scribbled on them. Then Pasquale gave me a push. It was showtime!

"Uh, first off, thanks for coming, everybody," I said. "It really means a lot to me."

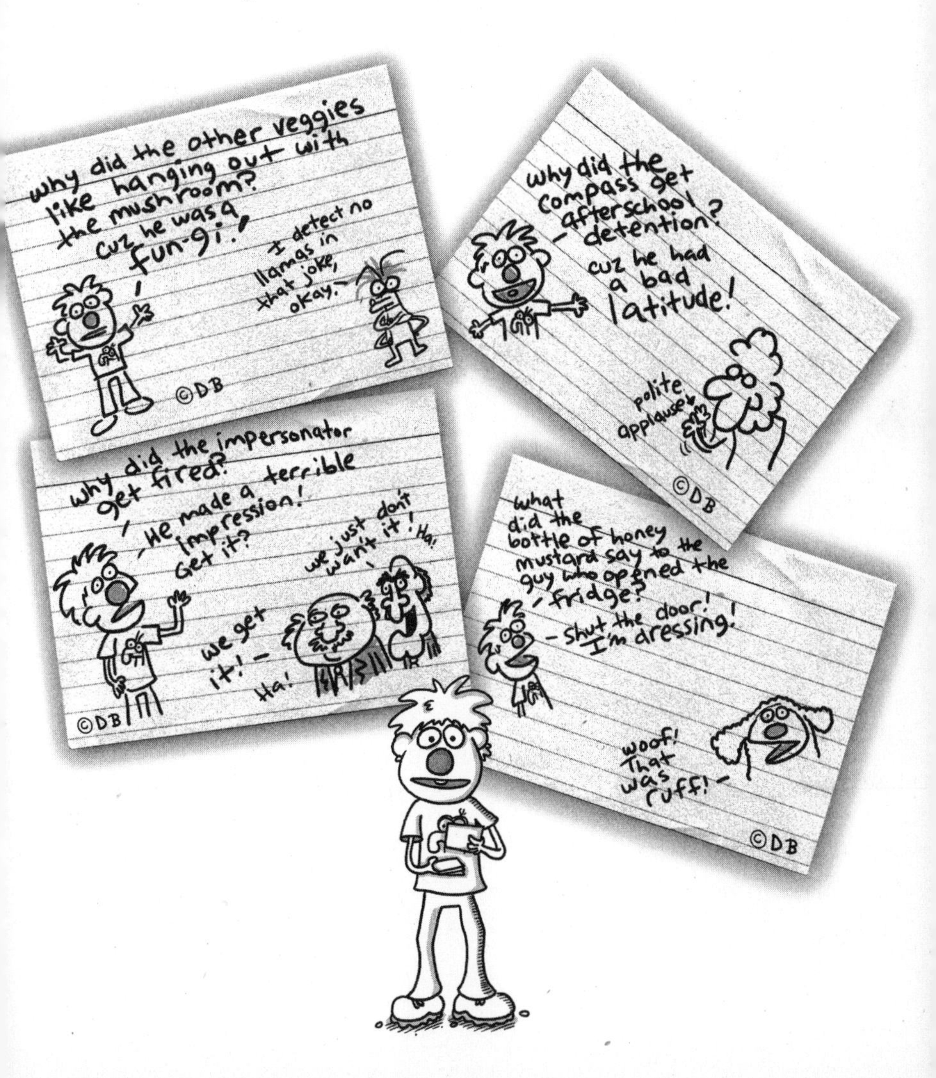

Ooooh, boy. My act did not go well. The rest of my jokes landed with an even louder thud.

When it was over, you could hear crickets chirping.

ACTUALLY, THE CRICKETS TOOK OFF AFTER THE SALAD-DRESSING JOKE!

At least Mom and Dad gave me some feeble applause.

"It's all right," I said, moping. "You don't have to clap. I know it was horrible."

"Thank goodness," said Pepe. "Because I find it very hard to lie, okay. Unless it helps me get free appetizers or electronic equipment, okay."

I looked over at Statler and Waldorf, who seemed abnormally subdued. "You guys sure are quiet. Don't you want to rip into me?"

"Actually, it was only half bad!" said Waldorf.

"And we slept through the other half! Ha ha!" bellowed Statler.

Kip patted me on the back and said, "I don't know why you're so concerned with being funny, anyway."

"It's just that Phips guy," I said. "He's not half as funny as he thinks he is, but he's got everyone eating out of the palm of his hand."

"Maybe he spread peanut butter on it," said Rowlf. "It gets me every time. It's a dog thing."

Fozzie tried to console me. "At least you helped me feel better about my act."

"Gee, thanks," I said, sighing.

Everyone was just about to leave when Pasquale blurted out, "Hope is not lost! When all else fails, there is always…science."

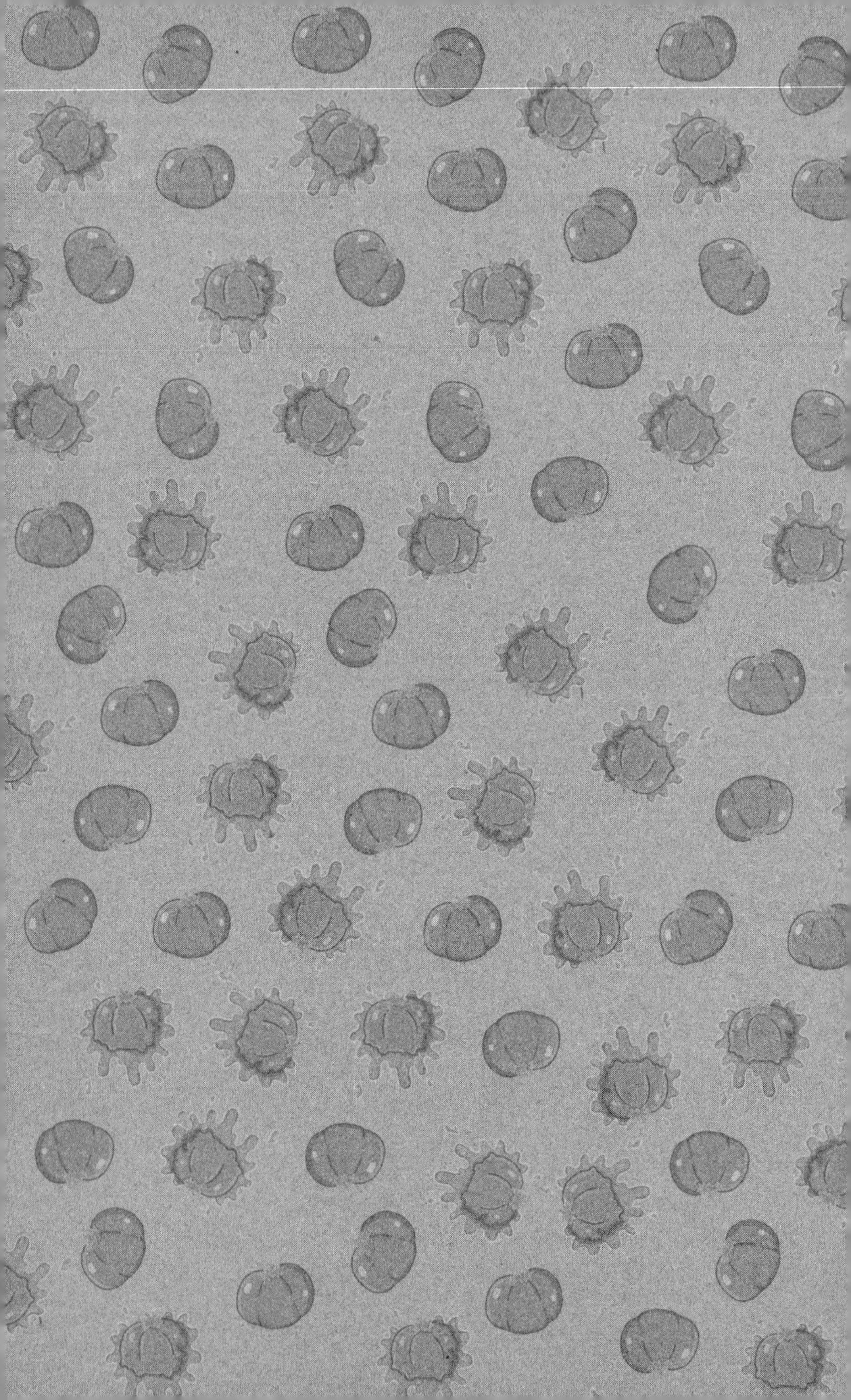

CHAPTER

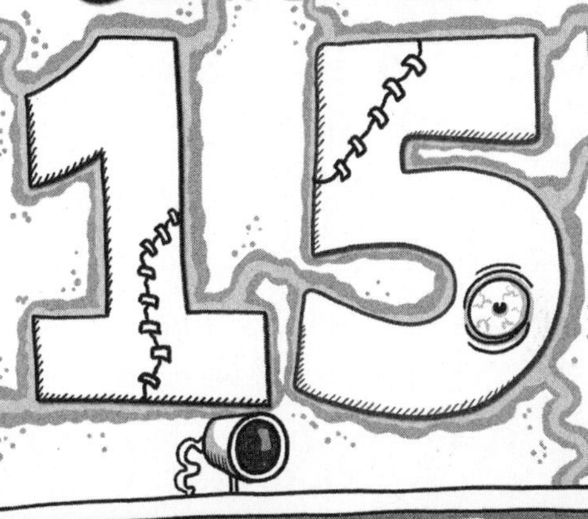
15

WWW.CRAZYMADSCIENTIST.COM
HYPNOSIS
MIND CONTROL
ESP
BRAIN FREEZE
DEJA VU
DIJON BLEU

"Dr. Honeydew," said Pasquale from the front of the room. "Remember the Deja Pew experiment from the other night?"

"How could I forget it?" asked the doctor.

Pasquale was so tired from all the hours of Angry Chickens and working on our single that he was starting to look like a mad scientist himself, with wild hair and dark circles under his eyes.

"I'm not sure what you mean," said Dr. Honeydew.

Pasquale whipped out a marker and started drawing a diagram for us.

WHAT IF, INSTEAD OF RECORDING SMELLS, WE RECORDED THE BRAIN WAVES OF ALL THE FUNNY MUPPETS HERE TONIGHT?
YOU DO REALIZE THAT YOU'RE DRAWING ON MY KITCHEN WALL?

"What do we do once we've recorded them?" I asked.

"We turn those comedy signals into sound waves, an electronic pulse that could be used to reprogram your brain—like hypnosis."

"Yeeeeeessss. Like the hypnosis," said Pepe. "I know I'm getting very sleeeeepy just listening to this, okay."

"I like the way you think, young man," said Dr. Honeydew. "I have extra electrodes."

"And I brought my laptop," added Pasquale.

AND I FOUND THIS OLD TUBE OF CHAPPEDSTIX IN MY POCKET.

"With some quick reconfiguring, we can be up and running in no time," said Pasquale.

"Just hurry it up!" snapped Waldorf.

"It's at least three hours past our bedtime!" added Statler.

Within minutes, Rowlf, Pepe, Statler and Waldorf, and Fozzie were all wired up to Pasquale's notebook computer.

"Commence the electrobrainmatic refibulation!" shouted Dr. Honeydew.

"I don't know what that means," said Pasquale.

"Press ENTER!"

Pasquale hit ENTER and the lights and TV started to flicker and buzz and Rowlf let out a howl.

"Are you okay, Rowlf?" I said.

YUP. JUST WANTED TO MAKE THE SCENE A LITTLE MORE EXCITING.

Suddenly, a green blast of electricity swept through the living room and everyone on the couch rose a couple feet off the cushions.

"This is just like the laser light show at the Grungy Kittens concert in 1983!" said my dad.

Then everything died down. "Okay!" announced Pasquale. "Looks like I successfully captured all of your rip-snortingly funny brain waves on this disk!"

"Now, how do we transfer it to Danvers's brain?" asked Kip.

"Just put it in his flip-top mouth and pwess his nose to play," suggested Chloe.

Pasquale packed up his computer. "No, I'll have to transfer it into an electronic pulse tonight. Maybe I'll turn it into an MP3—that way you can just listen to it on headphones, and voilà! You'll be the next comedy giant!"

"Or it could turn your brain into a baked turnip," said Pepe. "Either way, it should be fun, okay."

Suddenly I remembered our boy-band song. "Speaking of MP3s, Pasquale, you have to release our new single by midnight tonight!"

"I know. And I have thirty-two more levels of my game to get through, too," he answered.

Pasquale was starting to worry me. I was seriously considering an Angry Chickens intervention! But I kept my cool, since I still felt bad about deserting him when I had first gotten swept up in my boy-band fame.

CHAPTER
16

WHAT I WOULDN'T GIVE
FOR SOME SLEEP.

It was Friday, the big day. Not only was my new single with Kip supposed to be out, but my big comedy showdown with Phips was taking place in a little more than eight hours.

"Uuuuuuggghhh..." Pasquale moaned, shuffling toward me, looking like he'd spent the night sleeping in a cold tomb, gnawing on rodent skeletons.

"Pasquale, you look like a train wreck. Did you finish our single and get it posted to the Internet?"

"Yeeeeesssss..." he groaned like a caveman Frankenstein.

"Did you finish the brainwashing super-comedy MP3 that will turn me into a first-rate funnyman?"

"Yeeeeesssss..."

"Good! You can use it to transform me at lunchtime," I said. Then I leaned in and whispered, "Don't tell anyone, but I brought in someone special to help us today."

I unzipped my backpack, and Pepe jumped out.

WHEW! IT WAS VERY CRAMPED IN THERE, OKAY. I HOPE YOU DO NOT MIND BUT I LICKED THE PEANUT BUTTER OFF YOUR PB AND J. DON'T WORRY: I LEFT THE REST FOR YOU, OKAY.

"He's not allowed to be here," said Pasquale. "He should have one of those apple stickers labeled 'Visitor.' We could get in trouble."

"Relax, okay," said Pepe. "If a teacher walks up, I will just freeze in position and pretend to be a beautiful sculptured work of art, okay."

"Besides, you need someone who can promote tonight's main event, okay. Now, first things second, we have to hang more of these posters."

"Wait a minute!" I yelled, grabbing the poster.

"This can't be right!" I said. "Tonight, at my apartment? I thought we were having it at the Muppet Theater!"

Pepe grinned nervously. "Well, funny you should mention this. It seems that the theater is being treated for the bedbugs tonight. The whole place is shut down, okay."

"They aren't using poison on the little guys, are they?" asked Pasquale.

"Of course not, okay. This is a humane and dignified operation, okay. They are using only harsh language and insults."

"My apartment, huh?" I said. "Well, my parents *did* say I could have a few people over this weekend. I guess I'd better call my mom and see if she can pick up some extra Pizza Poppers."

The bell rang and we all zipped off to class—right after I zipped Pepe back up in my backpack.

It was about ten minutes into Mr. Piffle's class that I started to realize there was something weird in the air at Coldrain Middle School. It started with a random joke.

I don't think I had ever even heard Button laugh before, much less tell a joke. She was usually crying when she spoke to me (don't ask me why).

It wasn't just Button who was cracking jokes, either. A lot of the other students, and even Mr. Piffle, were throwing out zingers; there were impressions going on in the corner; and some sort of overall zaniness seemed to be taking over.

It was like half the class had lost their minds.

Pepe whispered, "This place is even crazier than the school of fish I went to as a young plankton, okay."

"It's normally not like this, I swear," I said.

Even Phips was weirded out. "What's going on today?" he asked. "I've been trying to work on my material for tonight's show, but everyone keeps distracting me with terrible jokes."

"Now you know how it feels," I said with a smirk.

"It's spooky," said Phips. "It's like everyone's been programmed to be a comedian. It's abomin*able*. They're incorrig*ible*. It's horr*ible*."

"Enough with the— Wait, programmed?"

As soon as class was over, I ran to find Pasquale.

PASQUALE! HAVE YOU NOTICED ANYTHING WEIRD WITH THE OTHER STUDENTS AND TEACHERS TODAY?
NO, EXCEPT GREEVUS AND SCRANT HERE HAVE BEEN TRYING TO TELL ME ABOUT FIVE THOUSAND KNOCK-KNOCK JOKES.
KNOCK, KNOCK!
NOW, PASQUALE, YOU SAY, "WHO'S THERE?" SAY IT! SAY IT!

I shook Pasquale by the shoulders. "I think you accidentally mixed up the two MP3s last night! Everyone who downloaded our new single expecting groovy tunes and smoldering jams was programmed to be a jokester instead! Quick, test out the MP3 you were going to use on me."

Pasquale pulled out his player, slapped on some headphones, and hit Play.

BABY, BABY, YO. YOU'RE LIKE POISON IVY ON MY HEART. ITCHY, ITCHY, YO...

I ripped the headphones off his head. "Well?"

He looked embarrassed. "Yeah, um, I guess I got confused. I blame that chicken game."

"Didn't you check the single before you posted it online?" I asked.

"Actually, I pressed the Upload button and then downloaded myself into bed. It was four AM. Why didn't *you* check it?"

"You know my dad's computer is from the Stone Age! The other day it took me three hours to download the letter *D*."

I heard Button's laugh echoing eerily down the hallway behind me. Suddenly, visions of zombie-kid comedians spreading across the city filled my head, and I took off running toward the office. "We've gotta stop this from spreading!" I yelled. "I'm commandeering the PA system!"

"Hey, dude," said Kip, walking up to us with Danny and Cody.

I ran to him and grabbed his arm.

"Kip! Please tell me you haven't downloaded our single yet!"

Kip looked at me funny, his skin pale against the dark rings around his eyes, which glimmered under his bangs. He was speaking in a Pepe accent.

YEAH, I DOWNLOADED IT, OKAY. I HEAR THAT IT IS ALREADY NUMBER ONE, BUT IT SOUNDED MORE LIKE NUMBER TWO, IF YOU ASK ME, OKAY.
TRÈS DRÔLE!
KNOCKITY KNOCK, YO!

Pasquale leaned in and whispered, "Kip must have gotten some of Pepe's brain waves when he listened to the single. This is all my fault. If I hadn't gotten so swept up in that video game and had paid more attention, none of this would be happening."

Inside, I couldn't have agreed more. But Pasquale was my best friend, so I just kept it to myself.

"Calm down," I said. "I'm sure it will wear off in no time."

But by the end of the day, it wasn't wearing off—it was getting worse. Everyone who had listened to our new song was acting like a brainwashed yukmeister!

I couldn't wait to get home and have some peace and quiet before the big comedy jam.

MAMA MIA! THIS IS GOING TO BE THE MOST EXCITING REALITY SHOW I'VE DONE SINCE *SQUIRREL HOARDERS OF ORANGE COUNTY*!
TRASH
ZOMBIE COMEDIANS! ALL RIGHT!

I DON'T THINK THEY COULD FIT ONE MORE THING IN THIS JOINT!
CHAPTER
I HOPE THEY LEFT ROOM FOR THE EVICTION NOTICE! HA HA!
17
TONIGHT! apricot COMEDY JAM!
THANK YOU SO MUCH FOR LETTING US PERFORM IN YOUR APARTMENT. I PROMISE WE'LL BE AS QUIET AS A MOUSE. YOU WON'T EVEN KNOW WE'RE HERE.
The MUPPETS
DANGER: EXPLOSIVE GAS!!!
QUIT SNICKERING!

I thought I could get some downtime before the big showdown. But there would be no relaxing for me. The Muppet crew was already setting up in my apartment for our comedy jam and Chloe's big number. When I walked in, Curtis jumped on my shoulder and clung on tight—he was a little wigged out by all the houseguests. I couldn't figure out how in the heck Kermit had convinced Miss Piggy to show up at our feeble apartment.

Don't worry, Piggy. The theater might be closed for fumigation, but we've found an amazing location for tonight's show!
Hmph!
It's right in the heart of Broadway.*
AL'S DRY CLEANERS
we clean Pants!
* The Broadway Apartment complex near Al's cleaners.
Where thousands of music acts have played.*
oh yeah! Righteous!
* on my Dad's old record player.
Raging Shrub
Loaded with European Acootra Accoutra luxuries.
venetian blinds
french toast
English leather ottoman
©Danvers Blickensderfer

My mom tried to catch me as I ran to my room. "Uh, Danvers, we need to talk...."

"Not right now, Mom!" I hollered as I swished by. "Chloe's going on in ten minutes, and then it's time for my big comedy blitzkrieg!"

IT WAS NUTS. OUR LITTLE APARTMENT WAS STUFFED TO THE BRIM WITH MUPPETS! CHLOE AND HER FILM CREW WERE PREPPING IN THE PANTRY.
MAYBE WE SHOULD RECONSIDER THE FIREWORKS....THIS IS A RENTAL!
I WANNA SEE A SHOWER OF SPARKS BEHIND THE LEETLE PRINCAPESSA DURING HER SONG!
DANGER: EXPLOSIVES!
TNT
HA! HA! HEH!
SUDS
DANGER
FIREWORKS
BAZOOKA
PASQUALE WAS HELPING KERMIT TEND TO THE JUDGES IN THE BATHTUB.
WHAT ARE THOSE?
THESE ARE ARGENTINEAN TUFTED PUFFINS, A NOTORIOUSLY HARD-TO-PLEASE SPECIES. THEY WILL MAKE PERFECT IMPARTIAL JUDGES FOR YOUR COMEDY SHOW.
MEH!
ICE

OUR KITCHEN WAS A NUTHOUSE. SWEDISH CHEF WAS BUSY PREPPING CONCESSIONS FOR THE SHOW.
ICE CREAM
GROCERY LIST
AIR POPPER
TØØDERSDEE VER SMAKEN DEE SPEESHLEEE-SPEECSHEL PØP-KERNCHICKY! BØRK! BØRK! BØRK!
UNHAND HER, YOU BRUTE!
MY PARENTS' ROOM HAD BEEN CONVERTED INTO MISS PIGGY'S DRESSING ROOM.
COMEDY JAM
MISS PIGGY IS RE-QUESTING A DOZEN SILK NAPKINS AND A FANCY FRANCÉ FIZZY WATER WITH LEMON.
WE HAVE PAPER TOWELS AND TAP WATER.
GOOD ENOUGH.
Miss Piggy
Do not disturb

DR. HONEYDEW AND BEAKER WERE JUST ABOUT TO STRIKE GAS IN MY BEDROOM.
WE ARE CLOSE TO STRIKING A HUGE POCKET OF OBNOXIS OXIDE, WHICH WILL MOST LIKELY ERUPT AT A MOST INCONVENIENT TIME, THUS PROPELLING THE PLOT TOWARD AN EXCITING CLIMAX.
GOOD THING YOU LIVE ON THE BOTTOM FLOOR.
DANGER: HIGH PRESSURE!
Danger Pelligroso
ND GONZO WAS GETTING EADY FOR HIS STUNT.
I'VE GOT A DELIVERY OF THIRTY FLAMING HOT-DOG CARTS. I'LL NEED A SIGNATURE.
SORRY, GONZO. THERE'S NO ROOM IN HERE FOR YOU TO DO SUCH AN ELABORATE STUNT. YOU'LL HAVE TO WAIT UNTIL WE GET BACK INTO THE THEATER.
WAIT? UH-OH!
HOT DOG

Fozzie ran up to me. "Hiya! Is our rising comedian star ready for the battle of the belly laughs? Wocka! Wocka!"

"Actually, no, Fozzie," I said. "It turns out that the brain waves we collected from you guys turned everyone who heard them into a comedy zombie. There's no way I'm gonna hook that up to my head."

"Wow!" said Fozzie. "I never realized my brain was so powerful. Come to think of it, Scooter and Animal and little Robin have been acting funny all day. Maybe they downloaded the song last night, too."

"Animal never gets past the 'knock, knock' part," whispered Fozzie.

I was bummed. "You see? The experiment was a failure. Now I'm totally unprepared for my act."

"Look, Danvers," said Fozzie. "You don't need to be reprogrammed to go out there. Quit worrying and have fun. Stress can cause hair loss—I know from experience."

"But you're covered in fur."

"Yeah, but you shoulda seen me in college."

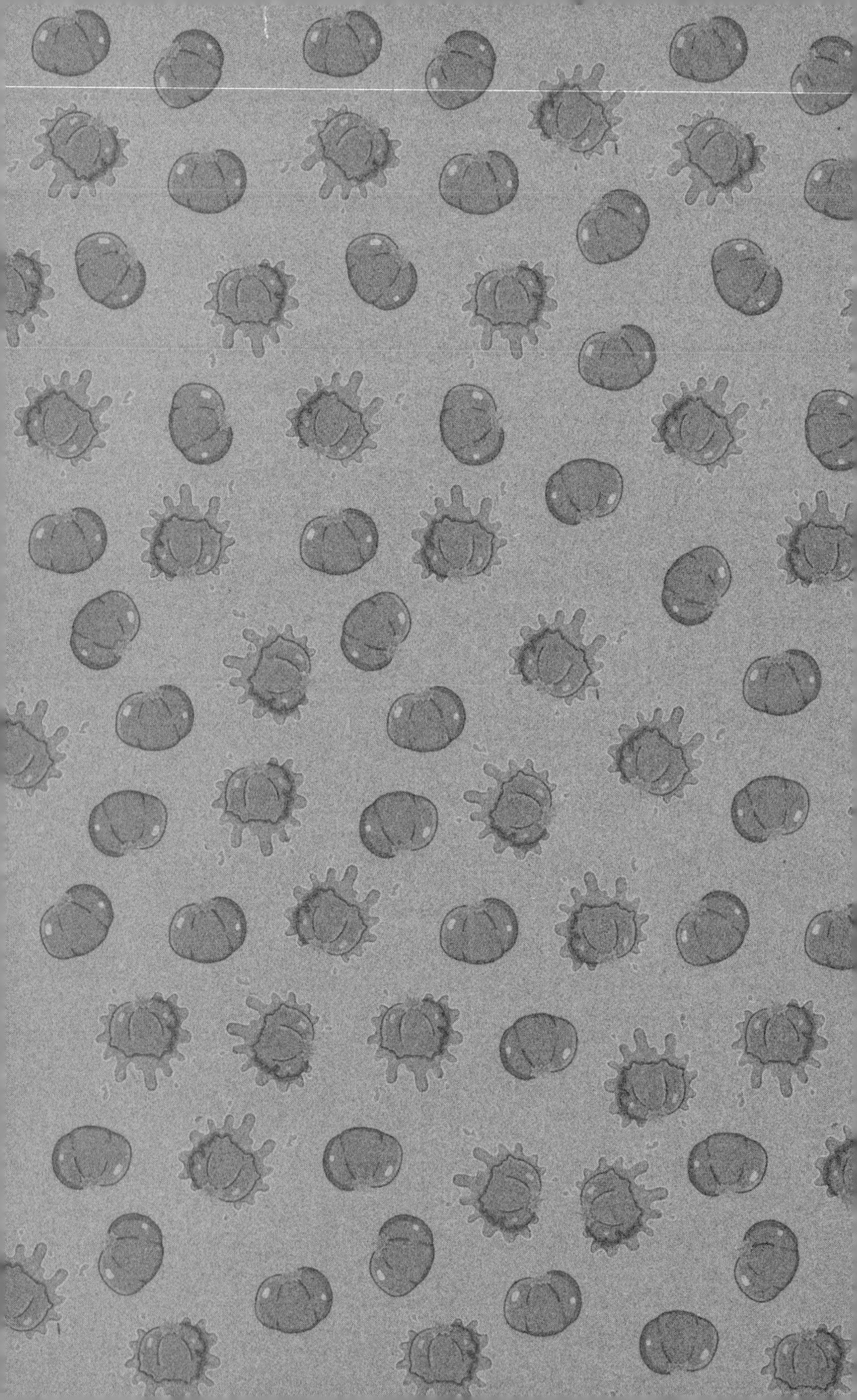

CHAPTER 18

COMING SOON

The show started off with a bang— literally. Crazy Harry's pyrotechnics backfired and blew up my mom's favorite potted tulips.

Kermit was frantically looking for The Electric Mayhem Band.

"Uh-oh," he said. "I forgot we need a drumroll for Chloe's introduction. Animal's too busy trying to tell a knock-knock joke, and the rest of the band's outside on the bus."

UND DRØØMROLL KERMIN UP!

"Thanks, Chef!" Kermit said, and then ran out and welcomed everyone. "Good evening, ladies and gentlemen! Thank you for joining us at the first ever Muppet Comedy Jam! As you can see, we've rolled out the brownish, splotchy shag carpet and spared no expense—because we didn't spend anything. I just hope everyone found a good seat!"

ARE YOU KIDDING?
THESE SEATS ARE TOP DRAWER!

Miss Piggy wheeled up beside me and Pasquale. She still had her cast on, and was getting pretty fast in the wheelchair. I was kind of surprised that she was willing to watch my sister steal her spotlight.

"Sorry about my little pill of a sister, Miss Piggy," I whispered. "I know you really wanted to perform tonight."

Piggy flipped her hair back and smiled. "*Moi* has

always been prepared for life's little surprises."

"Ladies and gentlemen and hard-to-please puffins!" shouted Kermit. "Let's have a big round of applause for our opening act, five-year-old singing sensation Chloe Blickensderfer! Yaaaaay!"

Applause filled the apartment, then died down as my little sis approached the mic holding a small sheet of paper.

"This is gonna be great," said Rizzo, capturing it all on video.

I WEGRET TO INFORM YOU THAT I HAVE JUST SIGNED A CONTWACT TO SING THE THEME SONG IN THE NEW MOVIE *FLUFFLEBERRIES ARE FWEE*. THEREFORE, I AM NOT ALLOWED BY LAW TO PWEFORM TONIGHT. I KNOW YOU MUST BE DEVASTATED. THANK YOU, AND GOOD NIGHT.

As she walked away, Mondo shouted, "Whadda dramatic tweest of events! Dis reality show ees gonna be more popular than *I Was a Teenage Grub Worm!*"

I turned to Miss Piggy and said, "Wow! What great luck!"

"Luck? Ha!" Piggy laughed. "I simply put in a few calls to the Fluffleberries' producers. Like I said, *moi* is always prepared. Hit it, boys!"

Suddenly, the room erupted in music. Pigs wearing tuxedos burst out of every closet, cabinet, nook, and cranny with trumpets, saxophones, and my mom's three-speed mixer.

Piggy jumped out of her chair onto gold-plated crutches and declared, "This one's called 'Bringin' Down The House'!"

"Uh-oh," said my mom.

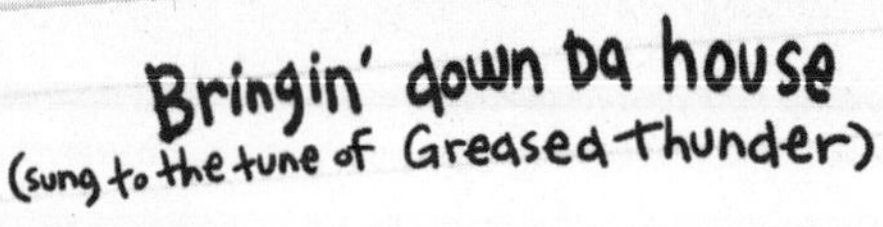
Bringin' down Da house
(sung to the tune of Greased Thunder)

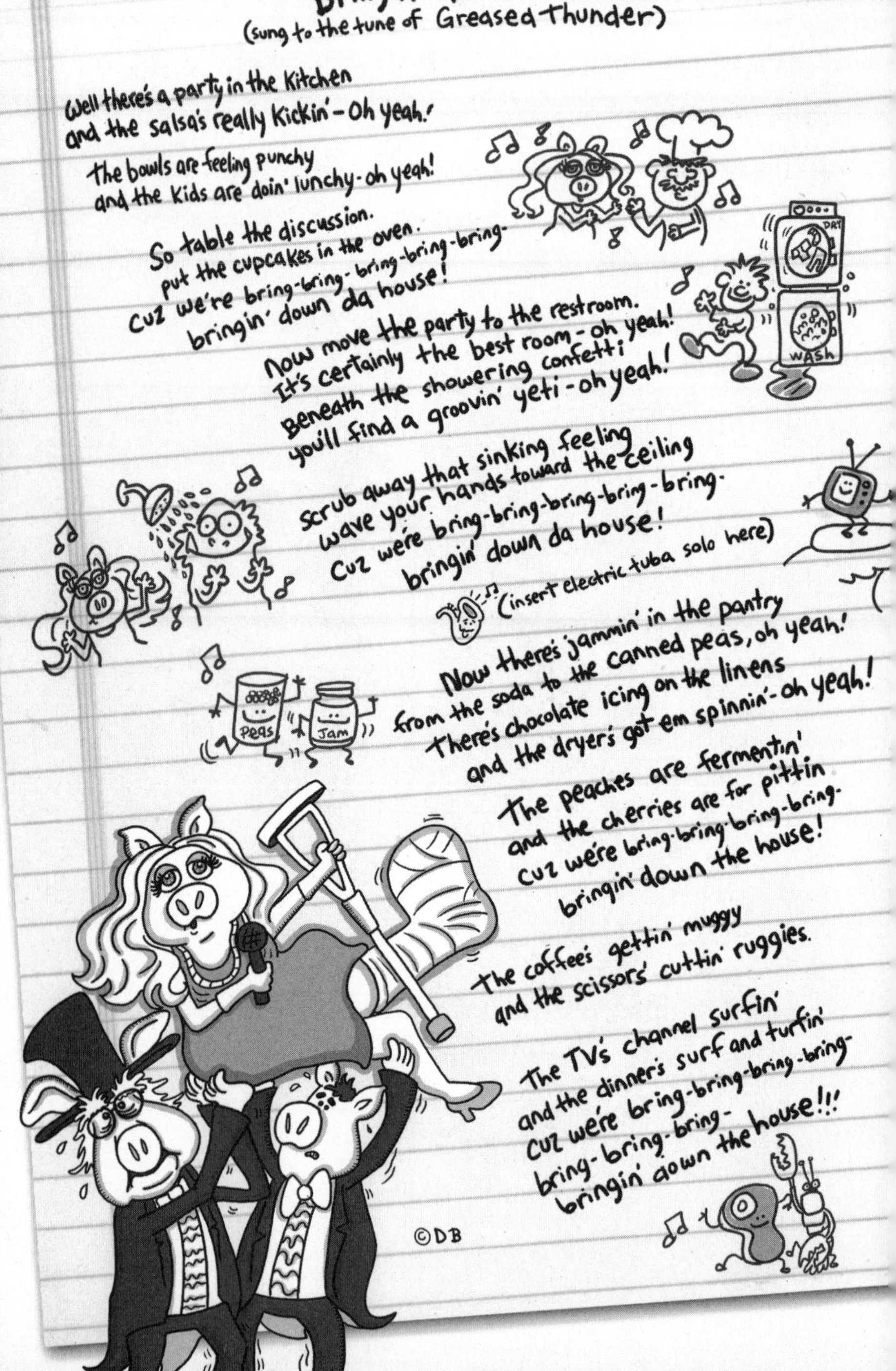
Well there's a party in the Kitchen
and the salsa's really Kickin' - Oh yeah!
The bowls are feeling punchy
and the Kids are doin' lunchy - oh yeah!
So table the discussion.
put the cupcakes in the oven.
Cuz we're bring-bring-bring-bring-bring-
bringin' down da house!
Now move the party to the restroom.
It's certainly the best room - oh yeah!
Beneath the showering confetti
you'll find a groovin' yeti - oh yeah!
Scrub away that sinking feeling
wave your hands toward the ceiling
Cuz we're bring-bring-bring-bring-bring-
bringin' down da house!
(insert electric tuba solo here)
Now there's jammin' in the pantry
from the soda to the canned peas, oh yeah!
There's chocolate icing on the linens
and the dryer's got em spinnin' - oh yeah!
The peaches are fermentin'
and the cherries are for pittin
Cuz we're bring-bring-bring-bring-bring-
bringin' down the house!
The coffee's gettin' muggy
and the scissors' cuttin' ruggies.
The TV's channel surfin'
and the dinner's surf and turfin'
Cuz we're bring-bring-bring-bring-
bring-bring-bring-
bringin' down the house!!!
DRY
WASH
Peas
Jam
©DB

When Piggy was done, the whole apartment went bonkers with applause. Even Chloe was clapping—something she usually only does when the lions catch a zebra on *Wild Planet*.

Kermit took the stage and said, "Wow! What an...uh, unexpected surprise. And a grand tour of Danvers's apartment to boot!"

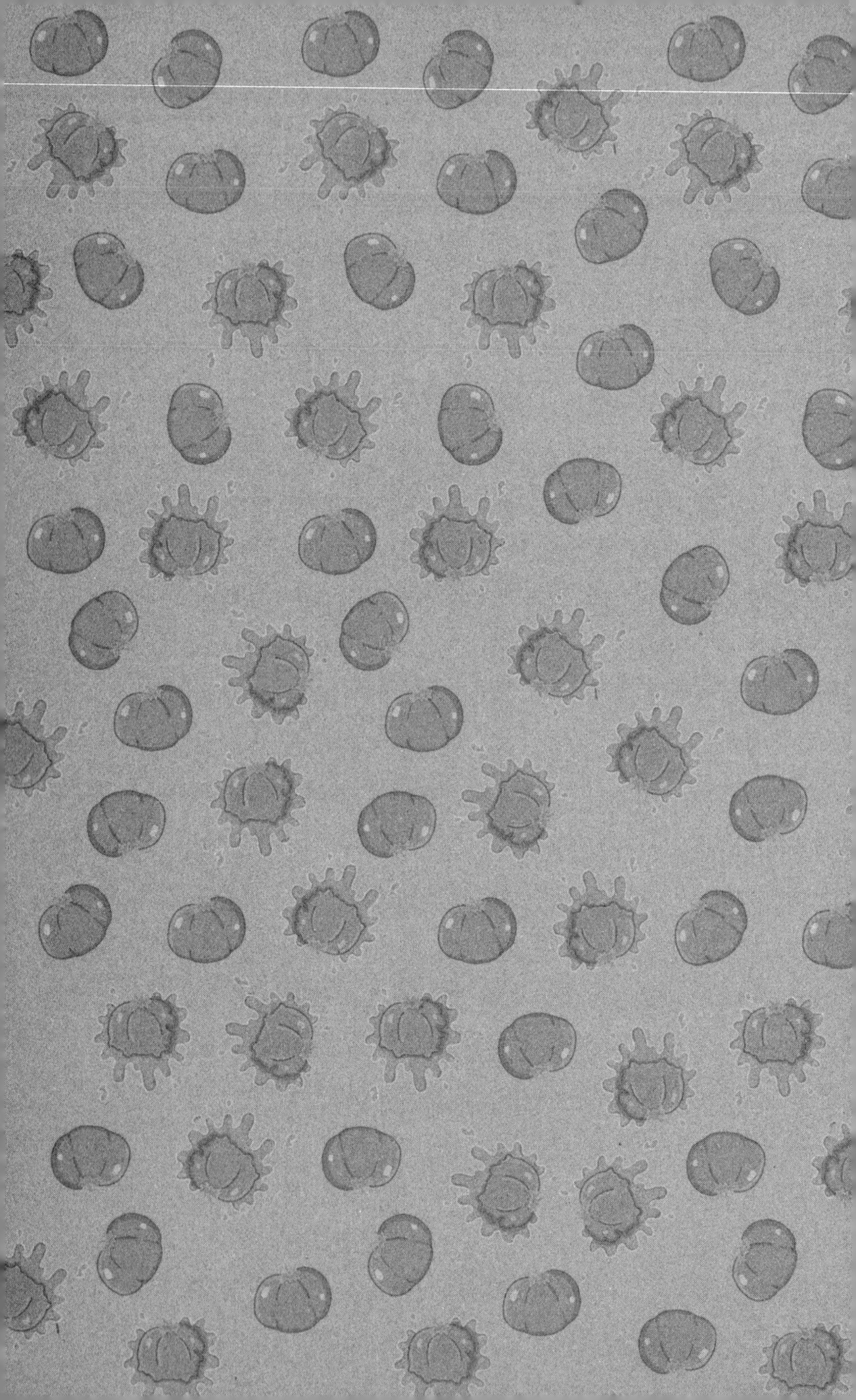

CHAPTER 19

ROUND
1

REMEMBER WHAT I TOLD YA, KID!
THAT PEANUT BUTTER AND BANANAS ARE GREAT TOGETHER ON HOT DOGS?
NOOO. TO JUST HAVE FUN OUT THERE!

It was showtime! Curtis lowered a microphone down from the chandelier to a funny-looking sportscaster with a pointy nose.

PRESENTING TONIGHT'S CONTENDERS! IN THE FAR CORNER, NEAR THE RED EASY CHAIR WITH THE STUFFING COMING OUT OF IT, IS CHALLENGER PHIPS TERLINGTON! AND IN THIS CORNER, NEAR THE IRONING BOARD WITH THE WOBBLY LEGS, IS OUR OWN WOBBLY-LEGGED DANVERS BLICKENSDERFER!

Swedish Chef made my mom's kitchen timer ding and the match was on!

Phips went first. It took him a little while to warm up, but by the end of his routine, the tufted puffins were definitely diggin' him.

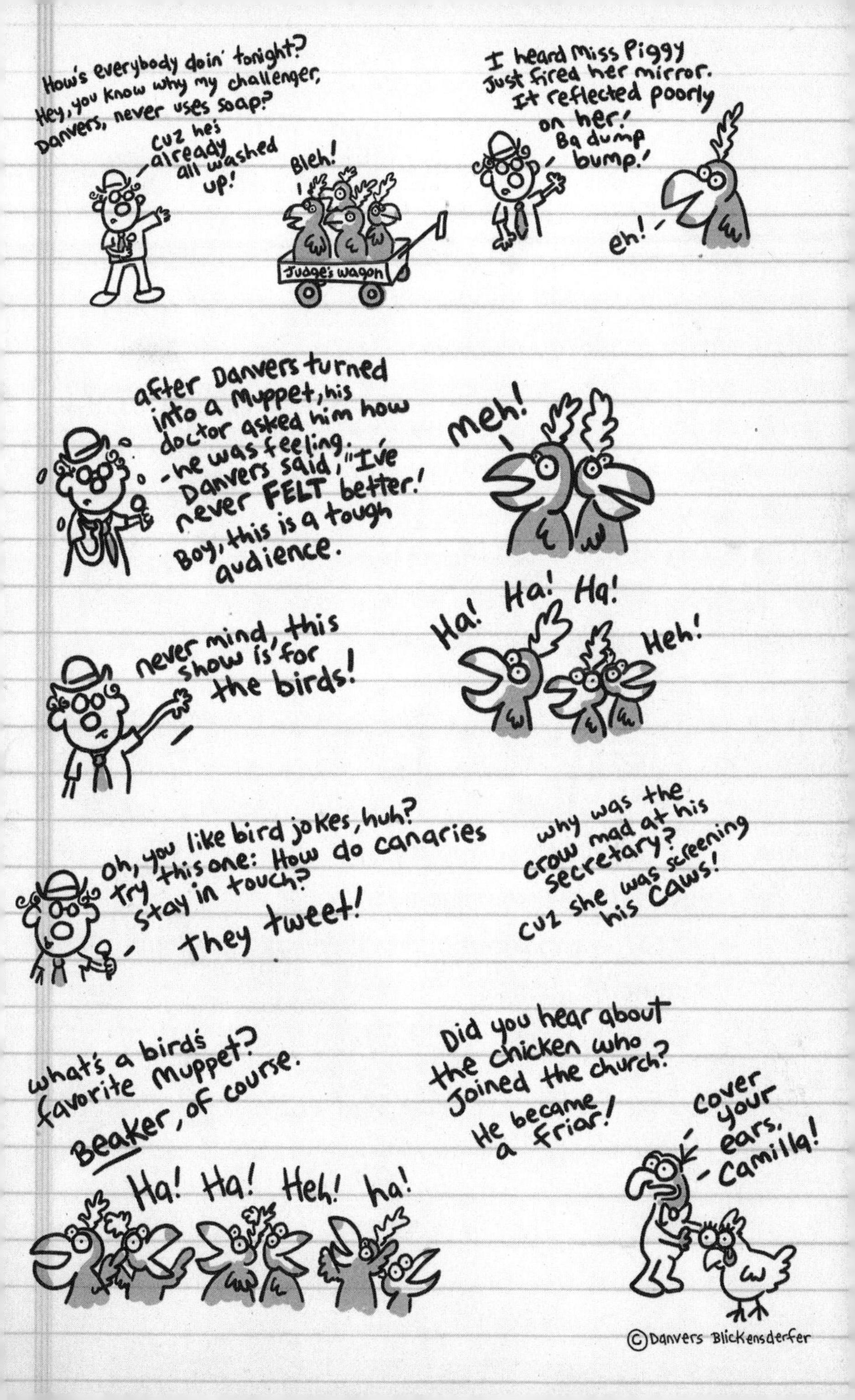
How's everybody doin' tonight? Hey, you know why my challenger, Danvers, never uses soap?
Cuz he's already all washed up!
Bleh!
Judge's wagon
I heard Miss Piggy just fired her mirror. It reflected poorly on her!
Ba dump bump!
eh!
after Danvers turned into a Muppet, his doctor asked him how he was feeling. Danvers said, "I've never FELT better!
Boy, this is a tough audience.
meh!
never mind, this show is for the birds!
Ha! Ha! Ha!
Heh!
Oh, you like bird jokes, huh? try this one: How do canaries stay in touch?
They tweet!
why was the crow mad at his secretary?
cuz she was screening his caws!
what's a bird's favorite Muppet?
Beaker, of course.
Ha! Ha! Heh! ha!
Did you hear about the chicken who joined the church?
He became a friar!
Cover your ears, Camilla!
©Danvers Blickensderfer

I was doomed. The puffins really liked Phips. I felt more nervous than ever.

"Try some bird jokes," my mom whispered.

"And when all else fails, do your flip-top mouth trick," added Pasquale.

PSSST! HEY, KIDDO. I BROUGHT YOU A SECRET WEAPON. I USED A JOKE FROM THIS BOOK TO CHARM YOUR MOTHER ON OUR FIRST DATE.
FUNNIEST JOKES OF 1982

I wobbled out into the spotlight—actually, it was just the light from the open fridge door.

"G-goo-good evening, l-la-ladies and gentlepuffins," I stuttered. "I'm..."

And that's all I could get out. I froze up.

There was complete silence in the room. Everyone was staring at me. Phips let out a snicker. Fozzie whispered, "Say something."

Curtis must have sensed my pain, or maybe he just momentarily lost his mind, because he suddenly reached over and nipped my removable nose right off my face like a ripe boysenberry!

"Hey!" I hollered as he stole my nose, leapt to the floor, and started running circles around me, holding my schnoz in his mouth like a dumpling.

There was a change in the puffins at that very moment. First a snicker, then a few belly laughs. And when I crashed into my mom's collection of ceramic owls, the whole judges' panel nearly had a conniption!

I finally snagged my nose back from Curtis and slapped it on my face, but at that point it was gross because it was all covered in lint and food crumbs. This made the puffins laugh even harder.

There was some snuffling as the puffins deliberated, and it looked like a sharp beak or two was jabbed in disagreement. Then one of the puffins waddled over, pulled out a fresh halibut, looked me and Phips over, then hurled the fish at my head. It smacked me in the noggin.

Suddenly, Kermit ran up and raised my arm, saying, "The halibut has spoken. We have a winner! Meet the new king of the class clowns, Danvers Blickensderfer! Yaaaaay!"

I couldn't believe it. Getting smacked with a raw fish was a good thing. I won! Curtis hopped back onto my shoulder.

"Thanks, little guy," I said, giving him a scratch under the chin.

He squeaked three times, which I think translates to, "No worries, dude. But you owe me big."

Phips even gave me a handshake. "Most commend*able*, Muppet Boy. I don't know if you won fair and square, but it was funny."

"Thanks!" I said. "You were funny, too."

A voice from outside cut me short. "Heeeeeeey-eelllllllp!"

All eyes darted to the front door as Pepe burst in, shivering.

WE MUST BARRICADE THE DOORS, OKAY! THERE IS SOMETHING OUT THERE. SOMETHING HORRIBLE!

CHAPTER 20

DANVERS, PERHAPS NOW IS A GOOD TIME TO DISCUSS SOME NEW RULES INVOLVING HAVING HOUSEGUESTS.
13
THIS SPACE FOR RENT

"What happened, Pepe?" I asked, shaking the little crustacean like a rag doll.

Pepe was trembling as he told his story. "It was terrifying. I was at the corner store, getting one of those egg sandwiches wrapped in the plastic, okay."

"That is terrifying," said Piggy. "Those things are disgusting."

"But here is where it gets really scary, okay. When I came back, the kids from Danvers's school started showing up one by two. Soon, there was a whole bunch of them, okay, and they wouldn't stop telling jokes. They were insulting me, telling the knock jokes, doing terrible impersonations of low-grade celebrities. We're talking C-minus list, okay. But I would not let them in, no matter what!"

"They must have gotten worse since school today," I said. "There's no telling what could have happened if they'd gotten in here."

"Noooo, Animal!" I shouted. "Don't let them inside!"

But soon the room was filled with an army of annoying robotic zombified jokesters. I saw Mr. Piffle, Button, Greevus—everyone who had heard our new single. Even Kip and the other members of Emo Shun!

The whole place was filling up, and the bad jokes were working our nerves.

"After this, I'm thinking of finding a new profession," snarked Phips. "Something joke-free."

"It's okay," said Kermit. "Just humor them. They don't seem to be violent."

"Yeah, I guess it could be worse, okay," added Pepe.

That's precisely when Dr. Honeydew ran in, screaming, "Everyone evacuate! We just struck Obnoxis Oxide gas, and it's going to blow any second!"

"I need to learn to keep my mouth shut, okay," Pepe said with a sigh as the whole joint started to rumble.

The front door was blocked by the horde of zombie comics, so I shouted, "Everyone, crawl out the kitchen window onto the fire escape! Hurry!"

Suddenly, green gas started pouring out of the back hallway, engulfing the zombies.

"Hurry!" yelled Kermit. "Cover your nose and mouth!"

Curtis clung tightly to my neck as I jumped out onto the fire escape. We lived on the first floor, so it

OUR LANDLADY'S NOT GONNA BE HAPPY ABOUT THIS.
HEY!
I THINK I JUST SPOTTED A GIGANTIC NEW PLANET THAT'S KINDA BROWN AND FURRY. OH, WAIT—IT'S JUST FOZZIE.

wasn't that far to the street below, but when I looked down, all I could see were zombies!

"Maybe we should climb up to the roof instead," said Pasquale.

"Yeah, dat's what I'm talkin' about, okay. Party on the roof!" hooted Pepe.

Pretty soon, we were all clambering up the metal ladder to the rooftop.

When we got to the top, I did a head count. "Is everyone okay?"

Miss Piggy let out a scream from below! "Aaaaah! Get back, you brainwashed gorillas! Kermie! Do something!"

I looked down to see Miss Piggy stuck about halfway up the ladder, her huge leg cast caught in the metal railing.

Kermit was valiantly fighting off the zomics with an umbrella. "Back! Back!"

"Oh, dear," said Dr. Honeydew. "It seems the Obnoxis Oxide has made the humorous horde even more unruly, demanding, and volatile. And I'm afraid it had nothing to do with your Muppetmorphosis, Danvers."

"My Muppetmorphosis is not important right now. We've gotta help Piggy and Kermit!" I shouted.

Chloe walked up and looked over the edge, then back at her camera crew. "Mondo!" she commanded.

Mondo tied his tongue to a flagpole.

OKAY, MONDO! TAKE US DOWN!
BROADWAY APARTMENTS
GRAB ON!
UP! MONDO! UP!
EEEGAH! IT'S SO HEAVEEEE! I DON'TA KNOW EEF I'MA GONNA MAKE IT!
DON'T BE SO DRAMATIC, LIZARD BREATH!
NOT BAD, KID. I OFFICIALLY NO LONGER WANNA TIE YOUR PONYTAILS TO A MOVING MERRY-GO-ROUND.
ARE YOU OKAY, MONDO?
MY THROAT IS A LITTLE SWOLLEN BUT I'MA ALL RIGHT!

Piggy and Kermit were safe, but we were all stuck on the roof, with nowhere to go!

"We're trapped like rats!" I shouted. "No offense to Rizzo and Curtis."

Pasquale ran over to the ledge and said, "The zombies can easily crawl up here!"

Swedish Chef ran up with a big pot of slop and started slathering the railings with it.

NOOOPE! NOOPE!
SLAPPIN DE GREASEE
MAKEE DEE SLIPPEE
SLIPPEE BOOMBOOM!
LARD

"Thanks, Chef!" said Kermit. "That'll hold 'em off for a while, but we still need to get help."

Pepe was already talking to the police on his cell phone. He turned to us and said, "Hey! Does anyone know another good story, okay?"

"What do you mean?" I asked.

"When I told the policeman that we were being chased by an army of gas-powered zombie kids telling bad jokes, he said, 'Tell me another one.' "

"What'll happen if they get to us?" asked Fozzie.

WELL, IT WON'T BE PRETTY. THE BRAIN CAN ONLY TAKE SO MANY AWFUL JOKES. ONCE IT REACHES WHAT WE SCIENTISTS LIKE TO CALL THE YUK THRESHOLD, IT WILL START TO SPASM, THEN JIGGLE, THEN TRANSFORM INTO QUIVERING BLOBS OF TAPIOCA PUDDING.
MEEP.
PUDD'N PALS

"Isn't there any way to reverse their condition, Doc?" I said.

"There is one minuscule hope. We could combat the affliction with Opposite Reverse Antonymium Therapy. But we would have to find someone or something that is the complete opposite of funny."

HAVE YOU TRIED READING THIS BOOK? HA HA!

"I think I might know someone who fits that description," I said, "but we'll probably have to bring him here against his will."

"Just trust me, Kermit!" Gonzo said, securing his safety helmet. "Hop aboard, Danvers!"

Curtis clung tightly to my shirt as I grabbed on to Gonzo. Pasquale jumped on, too. "I have a feeling you're gonna need me!" he shouted.

Gonzo shuffled to the ledge of the building, raising his arms into the air like a maestro.

ALL RIGHT, FISH! INFLATE THE YODEL BLADDERS!
THE PERUVIAN CATFISH SUCKED IN A TON OF AIR UNTIL THEY LOOKED LIKE BRATWURSTS THAT HAD BEEN ATTTACHED TO A BICYCLE PUMP. (DON'T ASK ME HOW I KNOW THIS.)
COWABUNGA!
ONZO LEAPT OFF THE ROOF AND WE PLUMMETED TOWARD THE GROUND.
YODADOO
KNOCK! KNOCK!
KNOCK! KNOCK!
KNOCK! KNOCK!
BIG FISH! BIG FISH!
THE FISH LET OUT A HIGH-PITCHED YODEL AS THEY DEFLATED AND WE BOUNCED RIGHT OFF THE ZOMBIES' HEADS AND ACROSS THE STREET!
WE'VE GOT TO GET TO THE BUS! JUST A FEW MORE BOUNCES!
YODELEYEEHOO!
SALUTATIONS, MY FLYING FISHY MUTATIONS! HOP ON BOARD!

Dr. Teeth ushered us onto The Electric Mayhem Bus. The Peruvian catfish immediately collapsed in the first seat, exhausted.

"I see you have *scaled* new heights," said Teeth, closing the door. "Now, if you'll kindly proclaim your destination, my young travelers of the cosmos!"

Gonzo gave me a confused look. "Where exactly are we going?"

I stood at the front of the bus and announced, "Eagle Talon Academy!"

CHAPTER

21
EAGLE TALON

DRATS! IF ONLY I HADN'T LEFT MY INFRARED NIGHT-VISION GOGGLES AND TRANQUILIZER CANNON AT THAT MOON-LIGHT LAWN-BOWLING TOURNAMENT.
HISTORY
FINE ART
MANGA

We snuck onto Eagle Talon Academy's campus and, sure enough, Sam Eagle was in his office.

"Boy!" said Pasquale. "Sam is really burning the midnight oil."

"But it's only seven thirty," I whispered.

"Dude, it's a figure of speech."

"Now, here's the plan," said Gonzo. "Danvers, you sneak in and douse Sam with this jar of bedbugs, then I'll distract him by juggling these pitchforks as I balance on top of a beach ball, so that Pasquale can throw a blanket over his head and you can swoop in and bonk him on the noggin with a honey-glazed ham!"

I shook my head. "I don't know, Gonzo. That sounds kind of violent. I say we use a much more lethal tactic—shameless flattery."

"Shameless flattery?" asked Gonzo. "Well, okay, that might work, but our young male readers aren't gonna be too happy."

I had to get Sam's attention, but I needed to be as gentle as possible so as not to startle him.

"Help us!!!" I shrieked, bursting into his office. "Heeeellllp!"

Sam screamed like a frightened narwhal!

HONK!
MY GOODNESS! DON'T YOU KNOW IT IS DANGEROUS TO SNEAK UP ON SOME-ONE WHEN THEY ARE BRANDISHING A CLOWN HORN?

"What are you doing here so late in the evening?" asked Pasquale.

Sam pointed to a poster of Buster Chapbuckle. "I was just rehearsing for my next Classics of Comedy class, since the first one was such a rousing success."

"Yeah, I could hardly be roused from my slumber when it was over," I said under my breath. Pasquale elbowed me in the ribs.

"It's terrific to see you again, Sam!" Gonzo beamed.

"I love what you've done with the place. Your collection of iron battle tanks is especially impressive!"

Sam looked at me and huffed, "Why did you bring that weirdo into my educational edifice? You do realize that despite my best efforts to instill a moral and patriotic rectitude at the Muppet Theater, this guy threw it all away to cavort with chickens and fire himself from cannons?"

Gonzo gave Sam a big hug. "That's right! I owe it all to you! Remember that patriotic bit we did with chickens surfing on jet fighters?"

Sam and Gonzo had a good chuckle—or, in Sam's case, a mild chortle.

TWENTY MINUTES LATER...
YES SIREE, THOSE WERE THE GOOD OLD DAYS.
THEY CERTAINLY WERE. WOULD ANYONE LIKE ANOTHER SLICE OF BAKED ALASKA?
SURE, I'LL TAKE ANOTH— HEY! WAIT A MINUTE! AREN'T WE SUPPOSED TO BE DOING SOMETHING?
HELLOOOO? THE ZOMBIES?

“Great Gossamer’s Goose!” shouted Gonzo. “I forgot the whole reason we came here. Sam, we need you to help us defeat an army of joke-cracking zomb—”

“What Gonzo really means to say,” interrupted Pasquale, “is that there is a large gathering of, uh, *students* who need an emergency lecture on the finer points of classic comedy.”

“At this hour?” Sam scoffed. “Children staying up past seven is a moral outrage! I won’t be part of it.”

“That’s exactly why they need you, Sam,” I added. “You can set them straight in the ways of comedy, bedtimes, proper etiquette when dining, and flag-saluting…everything!”

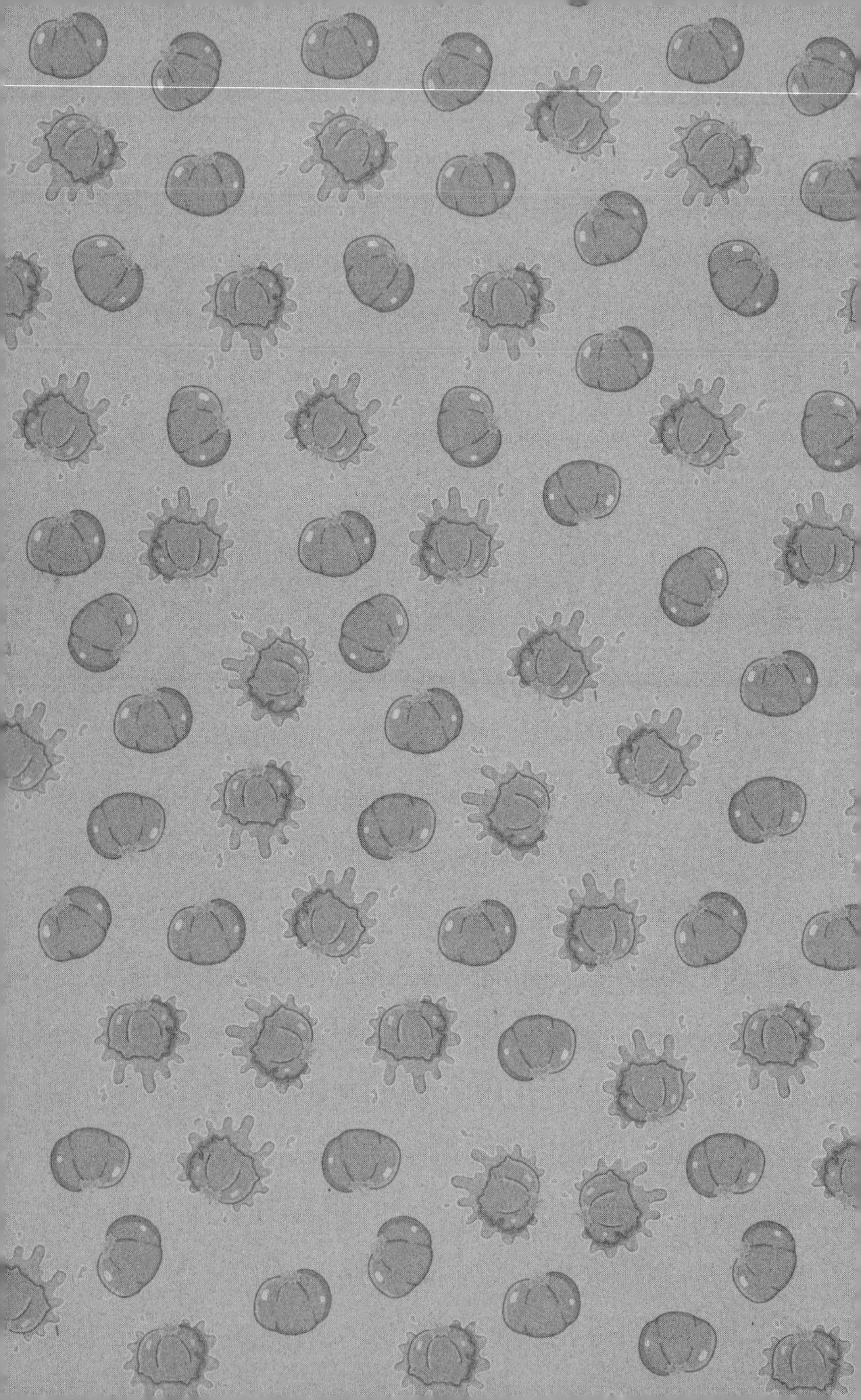

CHAPTER
22
SO, LET ME GET THIS STRAIGHT: THE NERDY KID USED OUR BRAIN WAVES TO TRY TO MAKE THE SCRAWNY KID FUNNY, BUT THAT PLAN BACKFIRED AND TRANSFORMED ALL THESE OTHER KIDS INTO ZOMBIE COMEDIANS WHO WANT TO TELL JOKES UNTIL THEY TURN OUR BRAINS INTO MUSH, AND NOW WE'RE TRAPPED ON THIS ROOF BECAUSE BEDBUGS INVADED OUR THEATER AND GONZO JUST WENT FOR HELP ON A PAIR OF FLYING CATFISH? WHEW! THIS BOOK'S GOT MORE PLOTS THAN A GRAVEYARD!
AND IT'S JUST ABOUT AS LIVELY! HA HA HA!
DRY CLEANERS
APARTMENTS FOR RENT. PRICES DROPPING AS WE SPEAK!

The Electric Mayhem Bus blazed through the streets, screeching around hairpin turns and hurtling over speed bumps at speeds in excess of 35 mph!

FARE TO MIDLAND
CAN'T THIS TUB OF BOLTS GO ANY FASTER?
ARE YOU KIDDIN'? THE ELECTRIC MAYHEM PUTS THE "BUS" IN "ROBUST"! THE "RACE" IN "BRACE YOURSELVES"! THE "OOMPH" IN "VAVOOMPH"!

I ran to the back of the bus to check on Gonzo and his bouncing catfish. "How are they doing?"

Gonzo looked worried. "Not so good. I think we wore them out."

"How are we gonna get past the zombie horde and back onto the roof?" I said.

Sam looked worried. "Excuse me—did you just say 'zombie horde'?"

Curtis let out a squeak, pointing at Pasquale's chicken game.

Pasquale suddenly shouted, "Of course! Curtis, you're a genius!"

He grabbed the game and started punching buttons.

"Uh, Pasquale," I snarked, "I don't think this is the time or place for video games."

"Oh, but it is!" He smiled. "Look! Level three hundred and twenty-two. You have to use a speeding bus to fling Gonzo in his chicken outfit over the crowd of zombies! Only in this case, we'll fling a stodgy eagle instead of an angry chicken."

"Sounds great!" said Gonzo. "We'll need a makeshift glider of some sort, and a giant rubber band."

"We can build a groovy glider out of these old Electric Mayhem Band signs!" said Floyd.

"And we can make a rubber band out of the bungee cords that keep the engine from, like, falling out onto the pavement!" added Janice.

We got to work as Dr. Teeth sped toward my apartment complex.

"Let's brake for launch!" Dr. Teeth shouted, slamming on the brakes just as Floyd released the bungee cord. We were instantly flung into the air like a mighty spit wad!

"*Viva el Pollo Libre!*" screeched Gonzo as we hurtled over the city street and the crowd of zombies. It was great—the sensation of flying, the cold wind blowing through my hair, my flip-top mouth flapping in the wind.

SCREEEEECH!
AAAAAAAAH!
THIS IS REMARKABLE. SAILING THROUGH THE AIR INTO BATTLE AS THE AMERICAN EAGLE WAS BORN TO DO! I HAVE REACHED NIRVANA.
CRASH!!
I HAVE APPARENTLY ALSO REACHED A BRICK WALL.
THAT WAS GREAT!
EXIT

I guess we misjudged the angle of launch.

"Quick!" I screamed. "Help me get Sam unstuck!"

We tugged Sam out of the rubble and put him in front of his makeshift podium. Time was short! The stand-up zomics had managed to make it past Swedish Chef's defense line of lard and were closing in.

"Pssst! Kermit!" I whispered. "We need an introduction!"

Kermit whipped out his bullhorn and announced, "Ladies and mindless zombies! You came here looking for laughs, and we just happen to have the king of comedy, the professor of pantomime, the sergeant of snickers—let's hear it for Sam Eagle! Yaaaaay!"

Kermit handed the bullhorn to Sam and the zombies gathered around him.

"Go on with your bad self!" shouted Statler.

"You're knocking 'em dead!" shouted Waldorf.

Sam went on to enthrall the audience with his theories on the hilarity of pulling your socks up past your knees, and, of course, Buster Chapbuckle's ability to make audiences...

I must have nodded off. In fact, when I woke up an hour later, I saw that everyone had nodded off—zombies included. Slowly, everyone started to wake up.

"Man!" said Rizzo, rubbing his eyes. "I can't believe I slept through the grand finale. That's not gonna make for exciting TV."

"We mighta have to adda some CGI effects to liven it up!" agreed Mondo. "Maybe throw in a half shark, half jellyfish."

"Yeah! Or a jellyfish-to-pus!" added Rizzo.

I saw Kip passed out near the railing and ran over to him. I was terrified he might still be a brainwashed wisecracker. I prodded him carefully and stepped back.

"Eeeyaaaaa!" Kip yawned, groggily coming to. "Dude, where am I? Why are we all on the roof? Does my hair look okay?"

The old Kip was back!

KIP! THANK GOODNESS! YOU'RE BACK AND NO LONGER ANNOYING!
WELL, I WOULDN'T GO THAT FAR, OKAY.

Sam had bored everyone back to their old selves. Mr. Piffle was cranky and humorless, Button was disgustingly adorable, and Scooter was chipper as could be. Even Animal was completely normal and calm…for Animal.

"No more jokes, please. I beg of you." Pasquale moaned. He looked like he needed three straight days of sleep.

Suddenly, Pepe ran up to us, waving his phone. "People! I just get off the phone with the lawyers, okay."

I strolled over to Phips and made peace. "You know, Phips, you really are funnier than me. I don't know why it irked me so much."

"Nonsense, Muppet Boy," he scoffed. "You and that rat have a bright future together. As bright as your crazy yellow hair and orange flesh."

"You might consider losing the 'ibles' and 'ables,' though," I suggested.

"Already done," said Phips. "Miss Piggy helped me make that decision earlier this evening."

"Sounds sensible," I said. "Maybe you'd like to join me and Pasquale. The school talent pageant is coming up, and I'm sure we could do some sort of cool comedy/boy band/extreme stunt spectacular."

"That's a great idea!" said Fozzie.

"Thanks," said Phips. "But I'm leaving Coldrain Middle School."

I was shocked. "Really? I guess your dad's being transferred again?"

Phips walked off with Sam. Pasquale mosied up to me. "I couldn't help but hear you guys talking," he said. "It's a shame he's leaving."

"Yeah, I guess." I nodded.

"Hey, Danvers," muttered Pasquale. "You wouldn't ever think of leaving Coldrain and going to Sam's Academy, would you?" He looked really worried.

I just laughed. "Ha! And miss Coach Kraft forcing me to climb a rope carrying a fifty-pound weight in subzero temperatures? Of course not."

"Whew," said Pasquale. "I was getting worried there."

I patted him on the shoulder. "No more worries tonight. And no more bad jokes! Now, let's go clean up this mess."

CHAPTER

23
GONZO
GONZO BMX BANDIT!
Let's Fluffle!
YOU'RE LUCKY, DANVERS. WE FOUND OUT FROM FURTHER TESTING THAT THE OBNOXIS OXIDE GAS LEAKING INTO YOUR ROOM COULD HAVE CAUSED YOU TO BE INCREDIBLY BELLIGERENT, CRANKY, DEMANDING, AND SASSY. I CAN ONLY IMAGINE THAT SOMETHING IN THIS APARTMENT MUST HAVE ABSORBED IT.
ARE WE GONNA GAB ALL NIGHT? I'VE GOTTA GET MY BEAUTY WEST, YA KNOW!

After the crowds of Muppets and former zombies had left, it was just me and Curtis on the top bunk, staring at my Gonzo posters on the ceiling. Curtis was having a late-night snack and soaking his paws.

"Well, Gonzo," I said. "Here we are again. The Obnoxis Oxide gas was a bust, and I'm still a Muppet. But what a day!"

"You got that right, brother," sassed Chloe, climbing up the bunk-bed ladder and holding up a poster she had drawn.

I sat up, furious. "'My Brother the Muppet'?! I *knew* it! You've been filming me the whole time, pretending that this show was going to be about you!"

"Hey, that's what our key demographic wants. You can see the story of a criminally talented young superstar like myself on any episode of *Tykes in Tiaras*. But a show about a boy who turns into a Muppet, gets a job with Kermit, transforms his school into a bunch of zombies, and saves the day with a pet rat, a giant chicken slingshot, and an eagle who gives lectures on pies? Now, that's a ratings bonanza."

I turned away from her. "Go away. I don't want to talk to you right now."

"Very well," said Chloe, climbing back down to her bunk and curling up with her Tickle Me Flufflеberry. "You'll be thanking me later."

How dare she invade my privacy and make a cheap buck on my painful story? Now I would have to come to terms with having my own reality show...my very own reality show, where I was the star, the hero who saves the day not once but twice. Where viewers could see me battling giant rats and zombies, doing insane extreme stunts with Gonzo, and singing smoky ballads to screaming girls. How dare sh— Wait a minute! This was starting to sound pretty cool. Maybe the little sister I thought was pure evil actually cared about me and was going to make me a star.

"Sis," I said, "thanks."

"No thank-you required," she said with a yawn. "I get sixty percent of merchandising rights, including T-shirts and flip-top Danvers saltshakers."

"Sounds fair," I mumbled, drifting off to sleep.

My dreams were filled with knock-knock jokes and zombies.

* * *

In the middle of the night I awoke to a strange sensation. At first I thought maybe I had seen another green flash. But the room was dark, and there was no smell of burnt pistachios and green apples this time. Chloe was snoring like an elderly wart-hog, and Curtis was twitching in his sleep, probably dreaming about being a rodent rock star and eating giant Cheezy-Qs.

I sat up in bed and sighed. "Must have imagined it." I was about to lie back down when a sheet of paper fluttered through the window. It blew across the room and lazily drifted down onto my bedspread. I held it up in the moonlight. It was the school enrollment brochure for Eagle Talon Academy.

I read the flyer from front to back, then laid my head down on the pillow and tried to go back to sleep.

But it was no use.

All I could hear was Phips saying, "It's the only school that can properly develop my creative talents," the words running over and over through my brain.

"Eagle Talon Academy," I whispered to myself. "Hmmm..."

WHAT HAPPENS NEXT? FIND OUT IN:

COMING SOON!

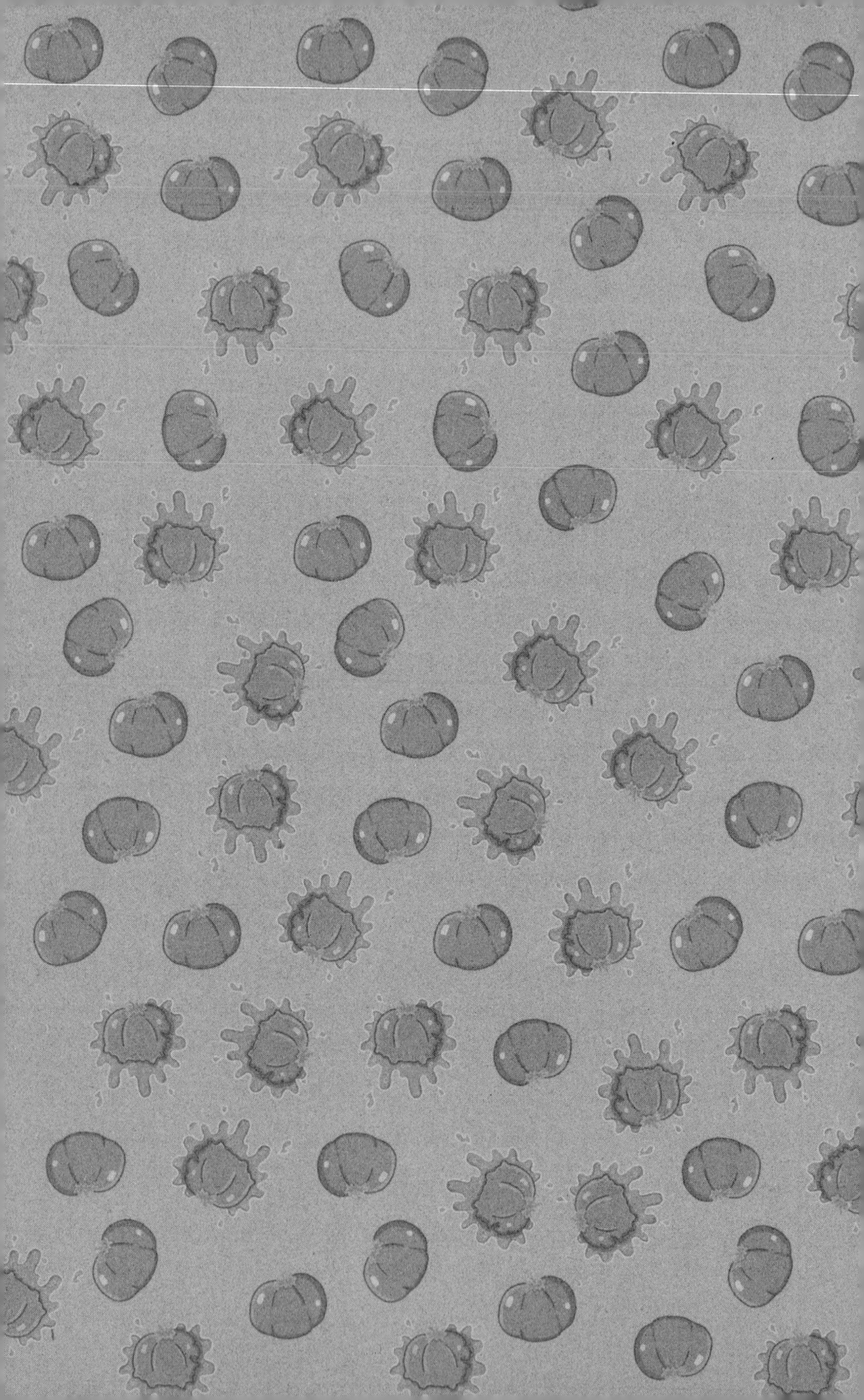

KIRK SCROGGS is rumored to have been raised by Muppets in the either the frozen tundra of the Yukon or the frozen food aisle of Kroaker's Groceries (historians aren't clear on this). What is known is that Kirk now lives in Los Angeles with an ungrateful cat named Chloe, eats steak with ketchup, and has sharp talons, which he uses to catch halibut and crack pistachios. You can find out more about Kirk in his autobiography, *Wiley & Grampa's Creature Features: Dracula Vs. Grampa at the Monster Truck Spectacular*.

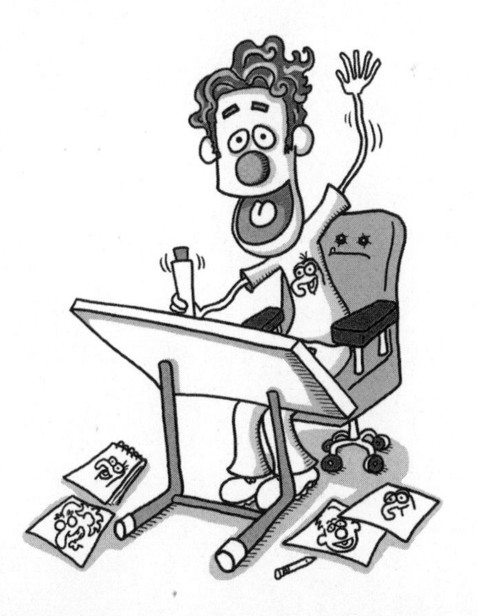

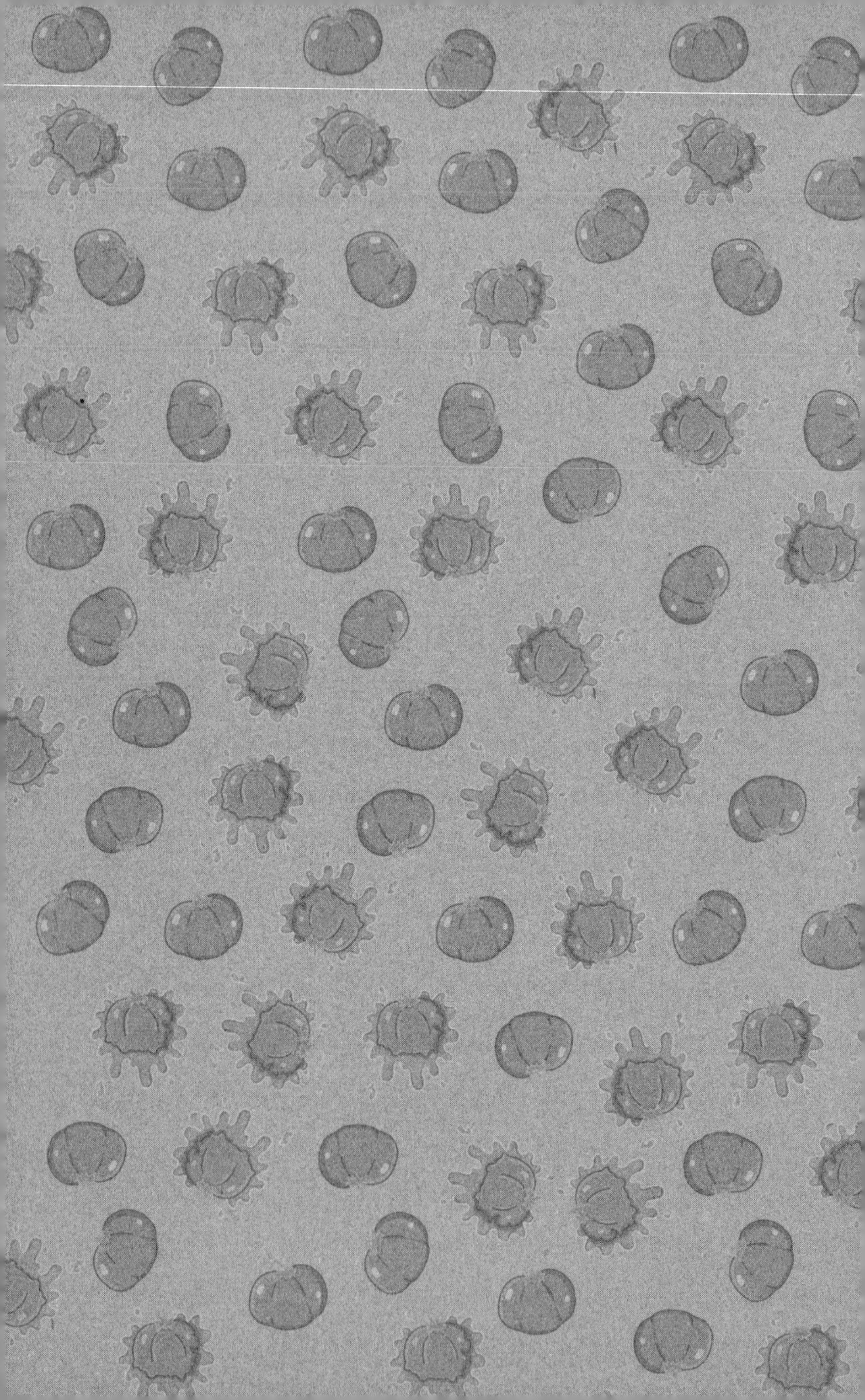

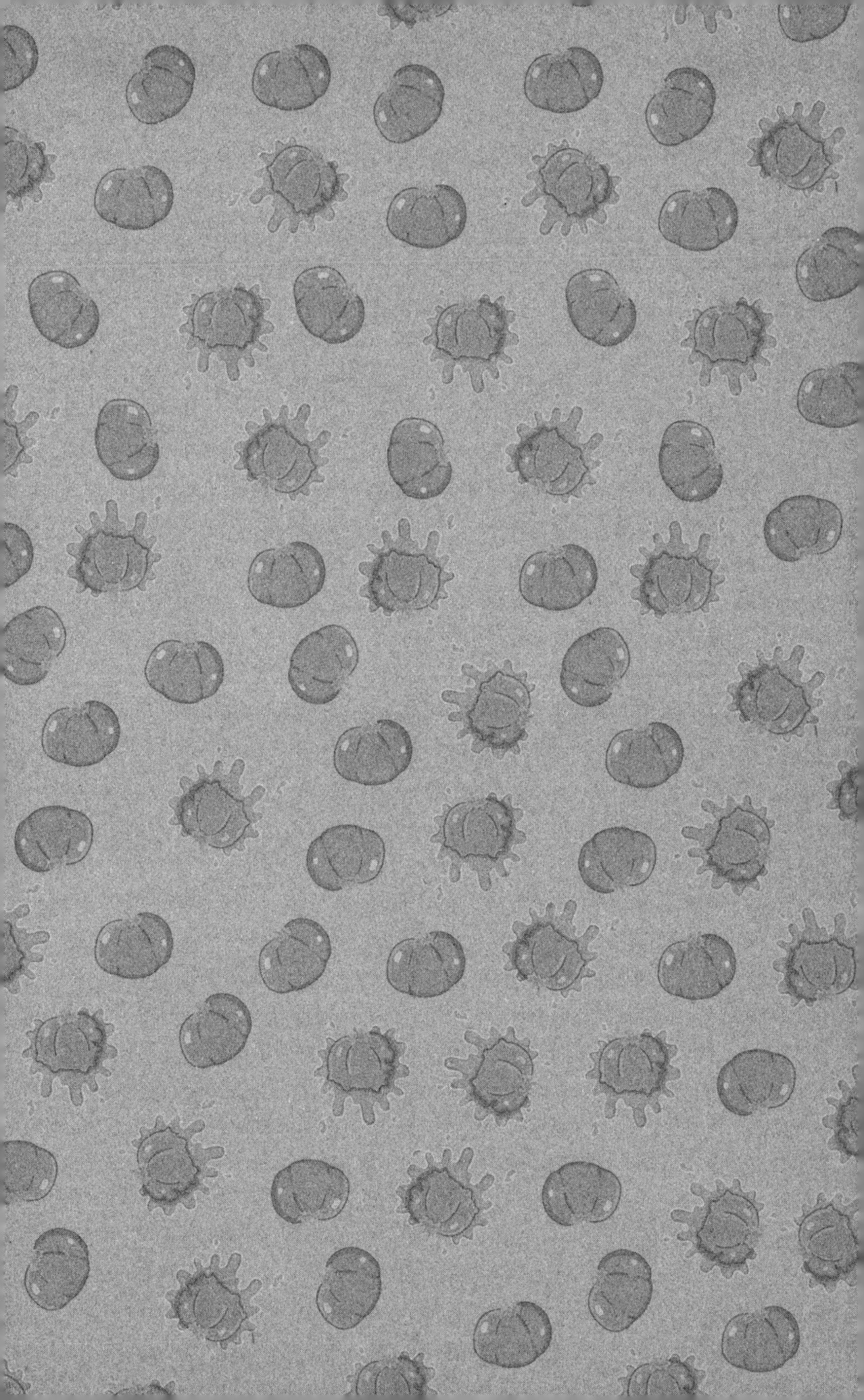

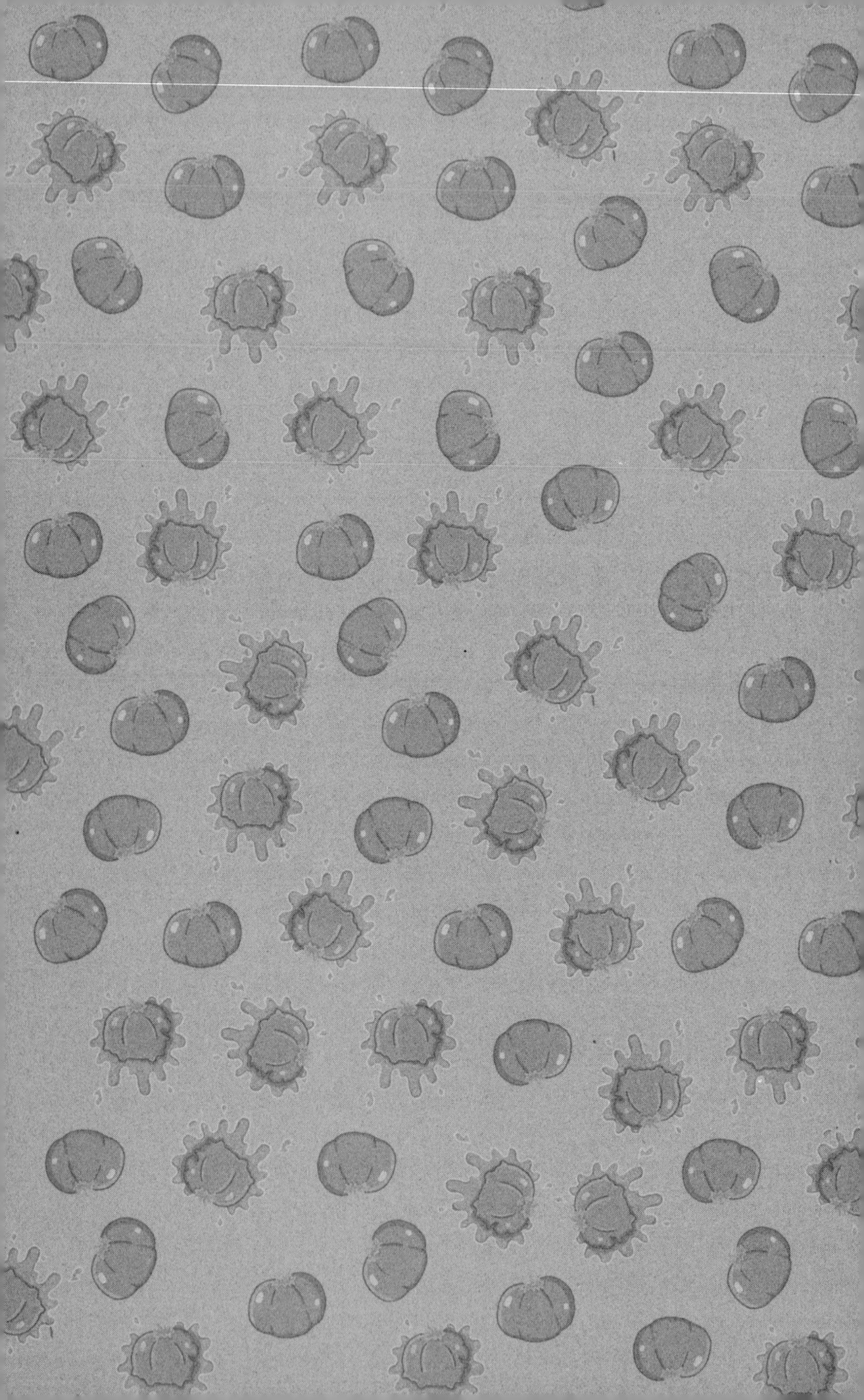

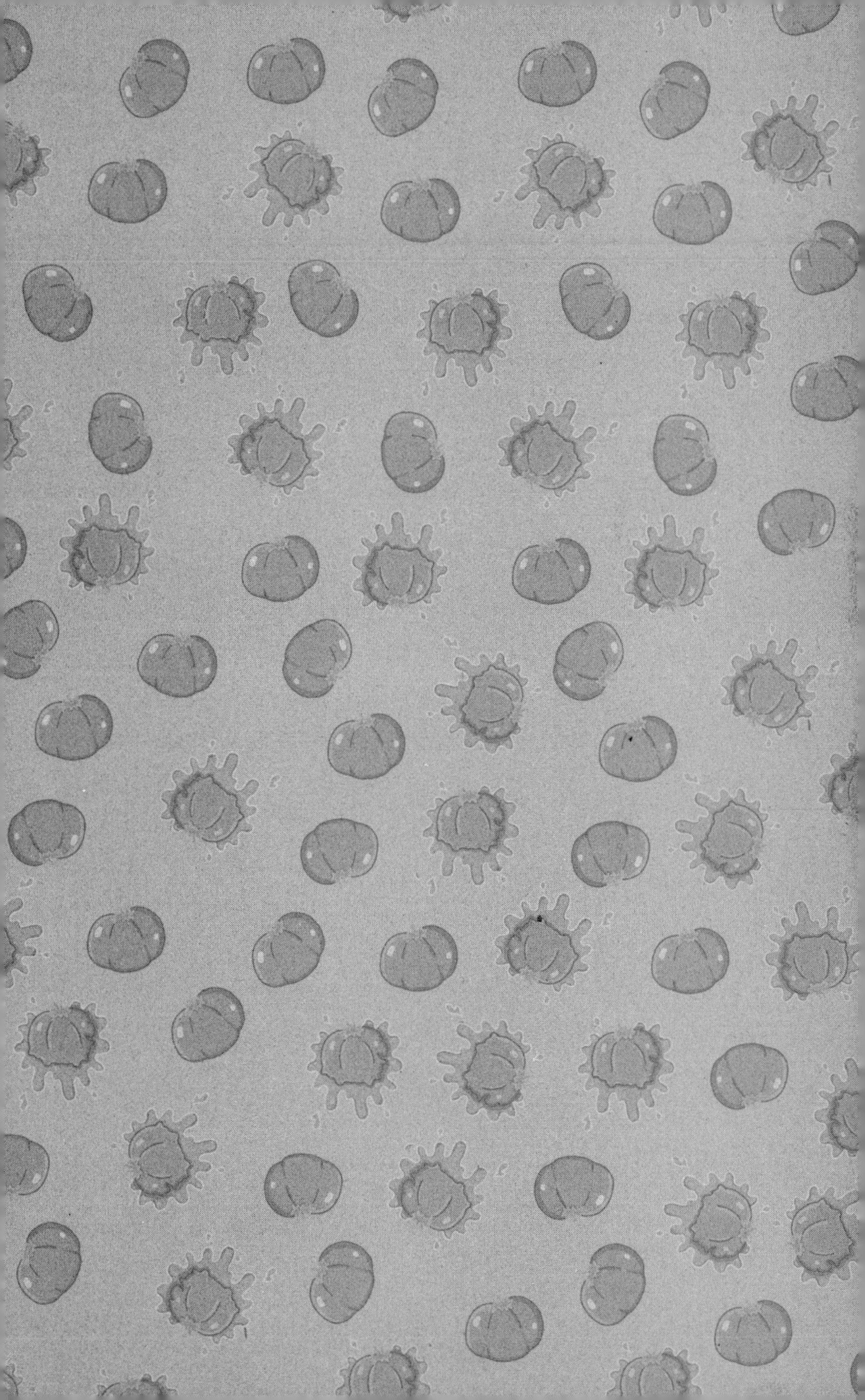

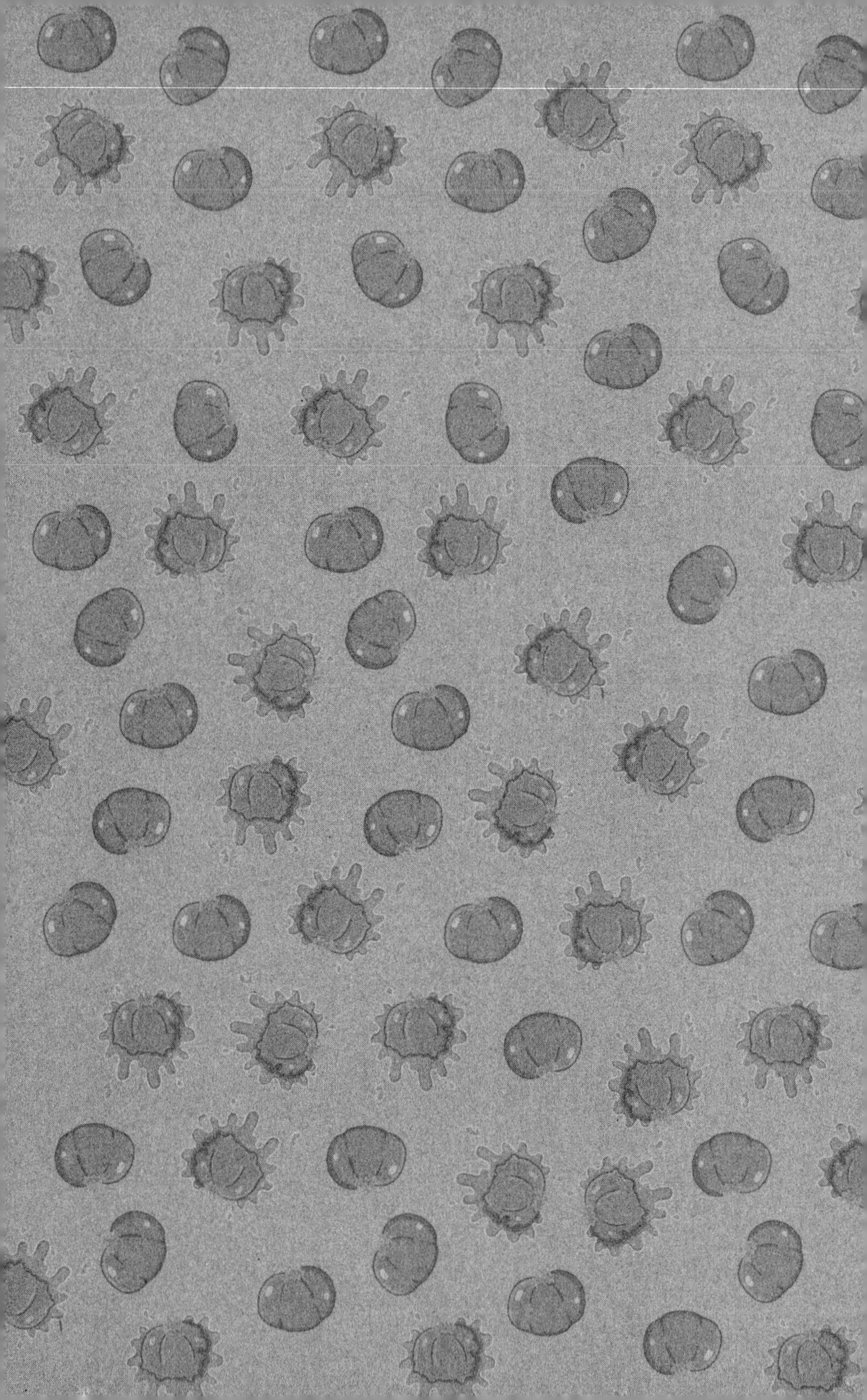

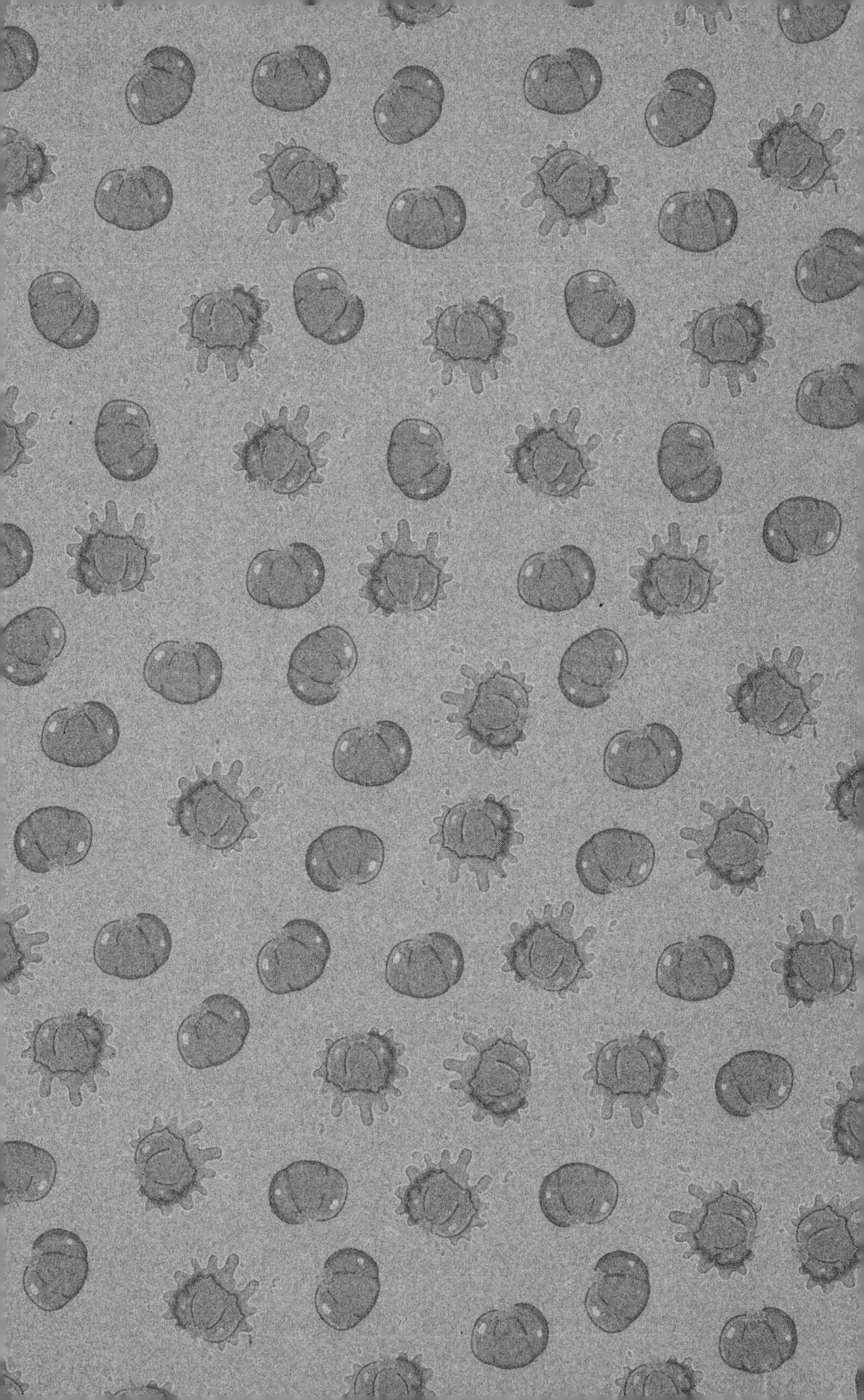

ITCHY ITCHY ITCHY, YO. SCRATCHY SCRATCHY SCRATCHY, YO...